GOING HOME

I love you
babe!
love Chri

GOING HOME

CHERI POPE

TATE PUBLISHING & Enterprises

Published by Tate Publishing & Enterprises, LLC
127 E. Trade Center Terrace | Mustang, Oklahoma 73064 USA
1.888.361.9473 | www.tatepublishing.com

Tate Publishing is committed to excellence in the publishing industry. The company reflects the philosophy established by the founders, based on Psalm 68:11,
"The Lord gave the word and great was the company of those who published it."

Book design copyright © 2010 by Tate Publishing, LLC. All rights reserved.
Cover design by Kandi Evans
Interior design by Joey Garrett

Published in the United States of America
ISBN: 978-1-61663-023-2
Fiction / Christian / General
10.03.02

"Greater love has no one than this, that he lay down his life for his friends."

John 15:13

BEFORE I START

My name is Robin Cane. I was sixteen years old. I died.

Everything was taken from me—stolen, whisked away right before my eyes. My family, my home, my friends, and my reason for being. I attempted suicide so many times, but there was someone who always stopped me; at least, they stopped me from physically ending my life. But no one could stop me from killing myself inside. So that's what I did. I killed my spirit, my heart, and my mind. Once they were gone, I started after my body. I fell into an abyss of loneliness and despair, my failure stabbing me and grinding me down. By that time, there was no one to stop me. There was no one to hold me back, no one to prevent me from taking my own life or letting something else take it for me. Except for one.

My name is Robin Cane. I am seventeen years old. I was saved.

I SHOULD HAVE KNOWN

I can't even begin to tell you how much it hurt. How my heart was violently ripped from my chest and stolen from me. How I couldn't breathe without coughing, eat without choking, or sleep without thrashing. I was being burned alive. Inside.

It had all happened so fast. Life had been moving on, just as it had always done, and then suddenly, it all changed. She was gone. She had been there forever, and then she was gone.

My mom used to be at home waiting for me to get home from school every day. Waiting with a special treat she had prepared just for me with the prettiest smile on her face, taking the attention away from the unexplained scarf covering her head. She'd scoop me up in the biggest and best hug in the world, kiss me, and tell me that she loved me more than anything, and then we'd spend hours together, playing card games, working together on my homework, having tickle wars ... and then one day I got home from school and she wasn't there. You can't imagine how that felt. I called for her, looked for her, hoping it wasn't what I thought it was. I found him. He told me where she was. We went to see her.

I hated it there. Everything was fake. Everything. The floors were too perfect, the colors were too pure, the windows were too shiny, and the people were too nice. What gave them the right to say anything? They didn't know her. They didn't care. They had already given up; they weren't even going to try. It was wrong. It was all wrong.

The first time I was there watching her lying helpless, sick, I stood frozen. Her face was the one thing I remember clearly, watching for me, waiting, trying to hide the fear, the pain. I had gone up to her and touched her yellowed, perfect face. I couldn't understand. I didn't know what she was saying. I got three minutes, and then he shoved me out of the room and stayed by her side for hours, as if I didn't exist. This became the usual routine. I didn't know why he wanted to be with her and not with me.

I was eight years old when my mom told me she was sick. I was eleven years old when my mom was first taken to the hospital and didn't come back. When I was old enough, I was able to go and visit her on my own, without dad. I'd go almost every day after school, not knowing if she'd be there when I arrived or not. I brought her flowers, I sang to her, I fed her ... she was my everything. Three agonizing years of chemotherapy, nausea, pain, and sadness passed by, and then she was gone. Just like that.

Like I said—I can't even begin to tell you how much it hurt when she died. But I can tell you this: it hurt even more when my dad couldn't stand the sight of me because I looked just like her.

Two years passed. I think he said maybe ten whole words to me in that entire time. Maybe a yes or a no. He faded away from me, drowning in his sorrow. I had just turned sixteen years old when I came home from school and found him lying in his bed in a pool of blood, gun in his hand. I remember I fell to the floor and sat for hours, staring at his lifeless body, wondering why he didn't love me as much as he loved her.

She didn't want to leave me here; she would've stayed if she could've, but the cancer was just too strong. But he—he chose to leave. He chose death over me. I wonder why I didn't see it coming. I should've known. After she died, he lost his will to live. I meant nothing. I should've known no one else could love me like she had. I shouldn't have expected anything from him. If I had just let him be, maybe he wouldn't have done it. Maybe he wouldn't have taken his own life. Maybe I'm just fooling myself.

He hated me. He hated me for living and her for dying. He hated me for being like her, for reminding him of her. Well, I hated him for letting her die. For letting me love her and then letting her die, and I hated her for making me believe someone cared, making me trust her, and then betraying that trust.

I would never let that happen again. Ever. If no one loved me, I'd never have to love back, and then *no one* would leave me or hurt me. No one. No one.

The day I decided no one could ever love me again was the day I really and truly started burning alive. Slowly.

POISONED BLACK ON THE INSIDE

I stared at it. The black coffin was slowly being lowered into the dirt, sinking into the seemingly bottomless hole. But as I was staring at my dad's coffin, everyone else was staring at me. I knew what they were thinking. They were pitying me. What did they care? Them in their expensive black suits and extravagant black dresses. They were the neighbours, the church members, the coworkers, the acquaintances. They were only interested in what happened to me now that I was left here alone. They'd been following our family's life story for years, and they wanted to know how it ended.

My mom, Tiffany, the star cheerleader, beautiful in every way, envied by all, married my dad, Marcus, captain of the football team, student body president, the most popular guy in college. They had the biggest wedding, the longest honeymoon, and the sweetest baby boy in the world. Me. Everyone loved us, wanted to be us … and then she got it. Lung cancer. They backed off. We weren't perfect anymore. Marcus withdrew, Tiffany deteriorated, and I turned into the dreaded, rebellious teenager who couldn't be controlled, or so that's what they said. But you know, if you get called something long enough pretty soon you turn into it.

And that's how they were staring at me. With pity, "poor kid," with curiosity, "What will he do now?" and with fear, "I hope they don't pass that piece of trash on me."

I remember thinking, *They can all drop dead for all I care. Just like Marcus. Just like her.*

"Hey, dude, how are you?" My best friend had approached me timidly. He didn't know what to say. I didn't blame him; I didn't even know what to say, but I had never been one for lying, and it certainly wasn't the time to start. "I'm going to kill myself tonight, Justin." I didn't look at him. I couldn't bear to see what was in his eyes.

He took my arm and gripped it hard. It hurt. "Don't say that. What good would that do?"

I knew he wouldn't let me. He had always looked out for me, like a big brother. But I didn't want him anymore. I didn't want anyone. "Leave me alone," I said. I walked back to the car the government had sent for me. I heard him call my name, ask me to stay and talk to him, but I just slid in the backseat and slammed the door. This time, I had a chance to save someone else from being hurt. If I made him think I didn't care, then he wouldn't be upset when I died.

"Your flight leaves at 5:25 tomorrow morning, Mr. Cane." The driver turned around in his seat and tried to get me to look at him. I didn't. I think I mumbled "Whatever," just so he wouldn't try to say it again. My mind started ranting.

Stupid government. They think they know what's best for everyone. They're making me leave my home, my friends, my memories. Relatives living in Canada? Screw them. I don't even know them. Honestly, making me fly halfway around the world for a bunch of people I don't even know, and who don't even know me, and who I'm pretty sure don't care. Florida is my home. It's always been my home. Why can't they just leave me here? Oh, that's right... I'm still a kid... too young to make my own decisions. Another thing they're clueless about. I've been making my own decisions ever since Marcus stopped caring. Ever since she died.

"I'll be here for you in the morning. Alice is inside," the driver said, dumping me on my driveway and speeding away. He hated me too. The first time he had seen me he stared in awe and then looked away in fear. Why? Did he have a problem with the way I looked? He hated my black hair. He hated my black clothes. He hated my black eyeliner. Hypocrite. He wore a black suit every day.

He can hate me, fear me even if he wants, but this is who I am. Black is just a color. He should just be thankful he didn't see what I am like on the inside. I know what I am; I know what I've been turned into. I'm not stupid. If he hates my clothes, let's see how reacts to the poison that's running through my veins.

"Hey, Robin. I made you your favourite." Alice, my personal slave, or that's what I liked to call her anyway, handed me a bowl of Kraft Dinner as I walked through the kitchen. They had sent her to watch me until they could get me out of there. Make sure I didn't do anything foolish. I guess they were smarter than I gave them credit for.

I snatched it from her and shoved her out of my way. "You only think it's my favourite because it's all that's been in this house to eat for years. If you weren't so stupid you would've seen that." I hated her—her smile, her thick blonde hair, her perfect skin. She was just like Mom. I never wanted to see that again. Why do you think I changed my hair and darkened my eyes? I hated looking in the mirror and seeing her face—the face that had caused my dad to kill himself. I had finally fixed it, changed the way I was so all I saw was my true self, and then she came along, ruining everything. I wouldn't let her touch me. Talk to me. Be around me.

"You know, I'm not that bad of a person, Robin. I'm just here to help you." She tried to touch my shoulder. She tried to hug me.

I slapped her hand away angrily. "Don't touch me! You want to help me then kill me yourself!" I seethed. No one wanted to give me what I wanted. No one would grant me my wishes. Wasn't I the victim here? Wasn't I the one they were all feeling sorry for? And yet I was the one they were denying the choice of what to do with my life. I wanted to end it, but that would not be allowed. They had already stopped me. Let me tell you now, getting your stomach pumped is *not* a nice feeling.

"Just stay away from me, witch!" I screamed and threw the bowl of noodles and cheese right at her face. I didn't stay to see if it had hit her. I didn't give a crap about her. I ran to my room and slammed the door as hard as I could, frantically searching for ways to get around Alice, to get what I wanted, but I knew there were none. They took all the pills from the house, all the knives from the kitchen, and anything that could be used as a weapon. And to top that off, Alice would be watching.

I sat down at my drum set, running my hand over the cymbals, trying to fuse what they felt like, what they looked like into my mind before I had to leave them. I remember swearing. Using as many bad words as I could think of and yelling them at the top of my lungs, I grabbed my drumsticks and banged on my set for hours, hitting each time harder than the one before. The sound was making my head hurt, everything else in my room was vibrating, and my arms ached, but I didn't care. It was driving me, pulling me down faster and faster until even if I wanted to I couldn't stop.

I don't know what time it was when Alice came into my room and tried to take the sticks from me. I flung them at her. "You want them? Take them! If fact, *take it all!*" I picked up the crash cymbal and its stand and heaved it at her. It landed on the floor with a loud rattle. One by one, I threw the drums at her, screaming the whole time. She didn't try to stop me. I scared her. Good! She ran out of my room, white as a sheet. I felt like I was changing inside as I continued to trash everything I could get my hands on. My heart. Something killed it and replaced it with something else. I don't know what it was, but it chewed at me. It burned me. It wanted to burn everything. My soul. I felt it shrivel and shriek as my rabid heart incinerated it piece by piece.

"Cane ... I'm going to have to ask you to calm down."

I turned around like an animal, wondering where the voice had come from, and wondering if I could destroy it. Alice had brought someone else into my room. A bodyguard. She stood behind the monster, watching me apprehensively.

"Get out! *Get out!*" I hollered while throwing whatever I could get my hands on.

The bodyguard came at me, and before I knew it, I couldn't move. He had pinned me down. "Come on, kid. You're going to kill yourself."

He was so stupid. Didn't he see that's what I was trying to do? I didn't even *know* it, and that's what I was trying to do. My torn soul and my mutated heart were trying to kill me, and I wanted them to succeed. I wanted it so bad. But I knew it wouldn't work, not with these goons always watching me. So I knew what my heart would do instead. If it couldn't kill me, it would kill whoever got in my way.

NOT YOUR WAY . . . MINE

"There will be an agent at the airport in Denver, just to make sure you get to your connecting flight," the bodyguard said. He hadn't left my side for hours, and now he was leading me to my gate through Miami International Airport. I had tried to get away from him so many times, but he always caught me.

"Whatever," I said, trying to yank my arm out of his sweaty hand.

"Not whatever." He swung me around in front of him and forced me to look in his eyes. "You have some serious problems, kid. Now I'm not saying you've had it easy, but if you keep this up, you're going to destroy not only yourself, but many people who care about you. And that's unacceptable. So you straighten out, or so help me ... I'll hunt you down and do it myself."

His overconfidence in his power over me was sickening. "What do you care? I'm just a paycheck to you." I twisted and pulled, but his vice-like grip on my shoulders only tightened, making me wince. I didn't want to wince. I didn't want him to think he had gotten to me; make him think he was making a difference. Unfortunately...

"I know you know I'm right." He tried to make his grating voice sound soft. "And I care because I've seen many punks like you ruin the lives of my loved ones and themselves. You think you're the only one that matters. The only one that's hurting."

"I *am* the only one! I am the *only* one!" I tried to kick him. I wanted to hurt him, to bash in his face for being so dumb. He thought he'd figured me all out, but he couldn't have been more wrong. No one else felt like I was feeling. No one understood what it was like to have the only people they ever cared about leave them. No one knew what it was like to have their soul die and their insides rot. I was standing in the middle of a crowded room, burning alive from the inside out, and no one would put out the fire.

He didn't say anything to me again. He just got me to my seat on the plane and then left, giving me one last pity glance. I gave him the finger as I shoved my backpack under the seat in front of me. Someone at the front of the plane started telling us how to put our seatbelt on and what to do if we crashed, but I didn't pay attention. *If* we crashed, it would've been a stroke of really good luck, and I wasn't having a lot of that lately. I felt my heart burning again, my breathing slowing, my fingers tensing as an annoying little girl with red hair sat down in the seat next to me. I looked around the cabin, trying to ignore her. The faint hum of the engine gave me something to listen to instead of hearing the idiotic arguments of the two people in front of me. Somehow, they had gotten the same seat. I looked out the window as the plane started taxiing across the asphalt, heading for the runway. Men in orange suits were running around, waving batons, getting out of the way, and driving shuttles. I wished I were one of them so I could run under the massive tires.

The airplane sped up and my stomach reeled. I held onto the armrests and closed my eyes. I hated the feeling that my insides stayed about a foot lower than the shell of my body, and the feeling that the air was being sucked out of my ears, crushing my brain. I wanted out. I looked around the cabin and spotted the emergency exit handle. It was right on the window of the seat ahead of me, red and obnoxious, calling me, telling me to pull it. I wanted to. I wanted to so badly. But the rest of the passengers ..., I wanted to end my life, not the lives of random, innocent people. I took my hand away from the enticing handle, took a deep breath, and rested it back on the armrest. The plane was levelling out.

Something touched my hand. I looked down at the little child who was running her grubby little fingers over the rings on *my* fingers.

"Why ... why do yoo have so manee wings?" she blubbered.

I tore my hand from the armrest, leaned down into her face, and hissed. She screamed and dug her scared little face into her mother's arm. I smiled as the frightened and enraged mom called the flight attendant over and asked to switch seats. The attendant glared at me and reluctantly led the mother and her daughter to the front of the plane, probably first class to make up for the horrors of sitting next to the deranged delinquent. I reached into my bag and pulled out my headphones, anxious to escape from the disapproving faces, the unbelieving expressions. I fell asleep.

I woke up when the plane touched down on the tarmac. No one was sitting next to me. I didn't blame them. I wouldn't want to sit next to me either.

"Ladies and gentlemen, welcome to Denver, Colorado." The pilot rambled about weather and tourist sites and about travelling with them again. I suddenly remembered, with disdain, the big, friendly agent who was waiting to escort me to my next flight to Edmonton, Alberta, where my mother's aunt and uncle lived. The last place on earth I wanted to go. Well, he could just escort someone else. My life was going to go my way. Not theirs. As I shuffled my way down the aisle with the rest of the passengers disembarking, I thought of strategies for my escape.

He obviously won't know what I look like. I can walk right past him and grab a cab. I'll just have to jump out before I'm supposed to pay him ... stupid cab drivers always ripping you off anyway. Then I guess ... I'll just find a bridge somewhere and jump off.

I had decided. As I walked into the meeting room with a slew of crazed families and friends who were excited to see their loved ones, I spotted him. Big, tall, wearing the black suit, and holding up a sign with my name scrawled in bold black letters. I slung my duffel bag over my shoulder and ducked my head while I walked right by him, trying to hide my smirk. I almost felt free, almost weightless, until I heard my name.

"Cane!" he yelled. I looked behind me. He was sifting through the crowd toward me, his eyes icy with annoyance. I took off. Where could I go that he couldn't follow? I darted through bookstores and duty-free shops, weaved in and out of lines, and dashed for the front doors. I could see the cabs just waiting for me. I was so close. So close I could smell the fresh air, see the mountains—and then all I could see was the floor. I gasped as I tried to recover from the two hundred pounds that had smashed into me and tackled me to the ground.

"Oh, man—you've crushed me!" I groaned, pain stabbing through my chest and my side.

He yanked me up and held my sweatshirt. "You little weasel. What did you think you were doing?" he growled, just like monster number one. "Think you could get away? Think I wouldn't catch you? I've been chasing criminals twice your size for years." He dragged me, struggling, down the airport hallways toward my next gate.

So I was a criminal now. *He* tried to kill me, and *I* was the criminal. What happened to juvenile delinquent? Possessed teenager? Troubled brat? Everyone stared as he towed me behind him, tripping because of the pain in my chest, and because he was walking too fast. "I think you broke something, you big ape!" I spat. He didn't turn around; he just yanked me along and shoved me down the bridge to the plane. I was the last passenger. The plane had waited fifteen minutes for me. Another wonderful reason for the passengers to give me death stares as I was forced into my seat.

"Now you sit here and be a good little felon." He sneered and threw a plastic bag of kids toys in my face. "Just play with your toys and color your pictures."

This right here is another one of those moments where I can't even begin to describe how I felt. If I had a knife, I would've shoved it in monster number two's back. He ruined my escape. Dehumanized me. Humiliated me. He was so lucky he left. I tore up the bag in pieces and threw them on the floor. The passenger next to me scolded me; the flight attendants warned me. I called them the worst names I could think of, put my headphones on, and went to sleep. Maybe when I woke up all of this would be a dream. Maybe I would be seven years old again, eating a salty soft pretzel after school, not caring about a thing in the world— or maybe I would still be in hell on earth.

PODUNK, ALBERTA

As much as I wanted to sleep the whole way, I didn't. I was woken up by the judgmental guy sitting next to me, or rather … on me. I couldn't sleep next to someone who had his head constantly dropping to my shoulder or his hands slipping and landing on my leg. It was the most annoying thing I had ever had to put up with. I inched as close to the side of the plane as I could, hoping he wouldn't be able to touch me. My mind wandered back to Marcus's funeral, when I had pushed Justin away from me. The look on his face when I said I was going to kill myself was etched in my mind. I closed my eyes and tried to remember a time when he hadn't looked that way. A time when everything was normal …

> "Can you try something a little faster, Robin?" Justin asked me as we tried the song for the third time and failed miserably.
> "Faster?" I said, twirling my favourite hickory drumsticks in my fingers. "If it's any faster you won't be able to understand the lyrics! Right, Ant?"
> Ant groaned. "I can't understand them now. Come on you guys … can't you just play simply, quietly? Does everything have to be so … epically hard?" He fiddled with his yellow dreadlocks as he fussed.

Justin picked a few light notes on his guitar. "Well, what if we went the opposite way and did it like this?" He looked at me, waiting for me to pick up a beat.

I jumped in easily, and the song flowed perfectly. "There … see? If we had just done it my way in the beginning …" I started to tease.

"Guys! Shut up! Just play!" Kiko yelled as he played some complicated riffs on his bass …

We bantered and played for hours in my room, just like we usually did. We were the strangest group of friends brought together in the strangest way. Justin was the neighbour who would hear me playing the drums at all hours and come over to tell me to shut up. One Saturday morning when he came over to yell, he brought his guitar instead and played along with me. We had the best time together once we discovered we had the same rhythms and playing style. It was his idea to start a band. We needed a singer, and he brought over one of his good friends named Ant, the typical Miami dude, usually high all the time, and completely obsessed with music and girls. He had the best voice I had ever heard, so he was automatically in for me. Then we needed a bass player, so we started looking around school and we found Kiko, a rich Hawaiian kid who moved frequently back and forth from Hawaii to Miami because of his parents' divorce. He was the best bass player in the school, and he never even had lessons. So our band was complete, and with the killer songs Ant would write, we knew we'd be famous someday.

But now they'll be famous without me because my life was torn apart, and I had to leave them.

I punched the seat in front of me. I had been trying to remember a good time, not remember something that reminded me of what was stolen away.

"Excuse me … do you mind?" The young woman sitting in the seat that I had punched leaned over to look at me. "I would appreciate it if you would stop bumping my seat."

I felt my chest burn again. "Screw you, lady. If you don't like it, move."

"Hey . . ." Her husband stood up and glared at me. "Don't talk to my wife that way, you punk."

That was the second time I had been called a punk that day. The fire crept up my throat and came out my mouth before I could stop it. "What are you gonna do about it, old man?" I said, sneering at him. "Beat me with your cane?"

He got out of his seat and reached for me, enraged. "How dare you!"

I stood up and shoved him as hard as I could before he could get a grip. "Back off, dinosaur," I heard myself say. I hated him. He was in my face, telling me what to do, what I should or shouldn't say. A few of the passengers screamed as he grabbed my shirt, fist raised, ready to deck me. I closed my eyes and waited for the impact, but when it didn't come, I opened my eyes to see another man restraining my assailant.

"Sir, I am a U.S. Air Marshal! Return to your seat immediately," he ordered. I smirked as the infuriated husband let go of me and spouted off to the marshal about what I had done. The marshal made him sit down, and then he turned to me. "Look, kid, sit down and shut up. I don't want any more trouble out of you." He pushed me down in my seat. "Okay?"

"Whatever," I mumbled. "They started it." I didn't look at him. I didn't want to see that familiar disapproving, exasperated look. Why did everyone have to be in my business? Why couldn't people leave me alone? I put my headphones back on, feeling sick to my stomach. Why was I always burning inside to kill everyone I talked to? I never used to be that way, but every time something happened, every time someone said something that bugged me, did something that annoyed me, I'd just snap and bite their head off. It was my blackened heart. I didn't care anymore about anyone or anything, especially not what others thought of me. If they judged me and condemned me by my appearance, like so many of them usually did, then so be it. I didn't need them. The one thing I knew for sure was that I would be prepared for anything and anyone. These new relatives I was going to live with, there was no way they were going to trick me or betray me like Tiffany and Marcus. I wasn't going to let them in so they could use me.

I wanted to yell it at him when we first met at the arrival gate in Edmonton, but he cut me off.

"Robin." The forty-something-year-old farmer extended his hand. "I'm your Uncle Eli. Eli Neufeldt. It's good to meet you."

I hated him as soon as he spoke. He was putting it on, faking it that he was glad to see me, to have me. I could see it in his eyes. He despised me. His eyes darted down to my bag. What did he want? Did he want to carry it so he could search it for drugs or guns? I bet he did.

"Well, we should get going. It's a good forty minutes to Two Hills." He put his hands in his tattered jean pockets and smiled.

Two Hills, I thought. *What is that? I thought they lived in the city. Oh no. He lives in a dinky, crap-hole of a town. Could this possibly get any worse?*

Eli's smile disappeared as he stood up a little taller. "Isn't it considered polite to at least say hello in America?"

It just got worse.

"I don't know," I said as icily as I could. "Isn't it considered rude to make fun of people in Canada?"

He watched me for a few agonizing seconds before he responded. "I wasn't making fun of you," he said quietly as he took my bag from me and started to walk away. I followed, trying to bore a hole in the back of his head with my eyes. Not only was he a grumpy farmer, he was the smart-aleck, know-it-all type who used every moment possible to analyze, patronize, and condemn. He grated on my nerves as he tried to act pleasant during the ride in his red, broken-down, rusted truck. It was like a running commentary about the weather, the road conditions, and his kids, whom I'd meet, and his wife's good cooking. Everything about him annoyed me. His plaid shirt sleeves hanging loosely unbuttoned, dirty and torn jeans, scuffed cowboy boots, unshaved face, and grungy baseball cap. Is this what Canadians were like? Uncouth, abrasive, and unkempt? I wanted to jump out of the truck and skid to a stop on the freeway, hopefully getting a concussion or something torn off. Like my head.

I let myself disappear somewhere else for the rest of the trip. There was no point in trying to avoid thinking about my mom and dad, so I didn't bother. What difference did it make anyway? Thinking about them hurt, not thinking about them hurt. Do you know how much energy it takes to loathe the very core of someone? How about two people who are dead so you can't do anything to them to relieve you of your hatred? Yeah, like I've said before so many times … you have no idea.

"Here we are," Eli said as we bumped along on a gravel driveway. For about two minutes, we had been driving through the smallest, dumbest, Podunk town I had ever seen. A barbershop, a grocery store, a church, and houses … nothing else. That's why it only took two minutes to pass through it. Now we were driving up to what I assumed was his farm in the middle of nowhere. His dirty, smelly, dusty farm.

"Goody," I grumbled as I got out of the rust-damaged truck and looked around. There was a large red and white house with a wrap-around deck, an old dilapidated barn with hay spilling out of the windows, and a stable that reeked so strongly I could smell it from where I was standing a few hundred yards away. Of course, all of this was surrounded by fields. I wish I could've cried at that moment, but I hadn't cried in years. It had never done me any good, so I had stopped trying. As I look back now, it's no wonder I was so angry. I had had no release. If only I could've cried. If only.

Eli put his hand on my back and ushered me forward to the line of people who were anxiously waiting to meet me. I shuddered at his touch and jumped ahead so he wouldn't have to push. "Robin," he said, "this is Martha, my wife."

The stout, round woman grabbed my shoulders and pulled my face to hers. "Robin!" She kissed my cheek. "Oh, you blessed thing! When I heard about my niece and then her husband, I cried so hard. It's a blessing to have you here, you poor thing." Her eyes glistened with tears as she held my arms with her pudgy fingers. I had already resisted the urge to throw up as she kissed me, and now I tried to resist the urge to knock her flat on her fat little bottom.

Eli continued his introductions. "This is Grandpa Joe; he stays in the cottage over there next to the barn." He pointed, but I didn't care to look. The wrinkly old man in a cowboy hat extended his hand to me and I took it, trying not to grimace too openly. He didn't say anything. He probably couldn't talk anyway. Eli nodded at Grandpa, who shuffled off to the house, mumbling under his breath. I think I heard the word *whippersnapper*.

"This is Eve and Esther, your second cousins," Eli said. "They're our twins." The two thirteen-year-old, redheaded girls stared at me, their eyes wide. I knew they were frightened, just like the little redhead on the plane, and I loved it. I narrowed my blackened eyes, glaring evilly at them, and they squeaked and ran away. Eli must've noticed, but he didn't say anything about it. Good.

A small gangly boy of about eleven tugged on Eli's sleeve.

"Of course . . ." Eli ruffled the boy's chocolate brown hair. "This is Caleb. He's my hard worker."

I watched as Caleb beamed at his father's compliment and then stuck his dirty little hand out to shake mine, his face disturbingly serene. I took it quickly and then wiped my hand off on the back of my pants. Who knows what he had on his grubby hands?

"And this . . ." Eli put his arm around the last person standing. A teenage boy at least forty-two years older than me and four hundred pounds heavier than me. "This is Israel. He's almost the same age as you, Robin. You two will have much in common. You'll be sharing a room. You can get to know each other."

I knew that was a joke. Israel's eyes alone told me that if I even tried to act on that he'd kill me, and his body language told me the rest. He at least wasn't faking. He looked at me like I knew how the others felt about me; like I was the worst thing that could possibly happen to him. He didn't want me here, and he wasn't afraid to show it with his menacing eyes and his tightly pursed lips. Eli gave him a look and left me alone with Israel as he and Martha went off to the house to get dinner on the table, or so they said. Israel's dark brown eyes stared me down, daring me to say something as he dragged my bag from the back of his father's truck and started towing it to the barn next to Grandpa Joe's cottage. I couldn't believe it. He slept in a barn.

As I forced myself to breathe through my mouth and not my nose, I climbed up the wooden ladder and looked around the loft. It was huge. It looked like any other room a guy would have, except everything was made out of wood or sticks. The sunset streamed in through the window in the middle, casting a somewhat archaic glow on the place. I almost felt myself like it, but then I quickly shoved that thought out of my mind.

"You sleep here," Israel declared as he threw my bag onto the bed in the right-hand corner. "And let me make something clear."

I dropped my backpack on the floor next to the bed and turned to face him.

"If you ever scare my sisters, bully my brother, insult my Grandpa, disrespect my father, or make my mother cry, I'll kill you."

"Really?" I said, staring right up at his stoic face. "If you ever scare *me*, bully *me*, insult *me*, disrespect *me*, or make *me* cry, I'll kill *you*."

He towered over me, his sun-bleached brown hair falling in his eyes, his jaw twitching, his huge biceps flexing. "Do you want me to make you cry right now?"

"Go ahead," I challenged. He was bluffing. I knew it.

"Listen, Miami. This isn't your world over here. It's mine. And if you think you can—"

"Miami? Wow ... trying to sound 'gangsta,' farm boy? Let me tell you something. I hate this country, I hate this place, and I hate you. So what makes you think I'll listen to anything you say about anything here?" I wanted to put him in his place, let him know right away that he couldn't push me around.

He pointed at my eyeliner in disgust. "Why do you wear this?

Hmm? You like the way it looks? Or are you trying to get everyone to hate you?"

I didn't have anything to say. He wasn't backing down, and it made me nervous. I was going to punch him. To kick him where it hurt, but Eli suddenly appeared beside us. "It's time for dinner, boys ... if you're hungry."

"I'm not," I said as I pushed past the two of them and ran out of the barn. I ran for a long time, looking for somewhere I could go, but all there was to see were fields. Endless fields of grain or straw or whatever the heck it was. I grabbed a stick and whacked at it, destroying as much of it as I could.

Screw this place, and screw these hillbillies. I'm getting out of here tonight.

REMEMBERING HER

I headed back just as the sun was going down. As much as I didn't want to admit it, I had never seen a more impressive sunset. Orange, yellow, purple, pink … It reminded me of my mom's oil paints when she would mix them together to paint her canvases. That's what she used to do. She was an artist.

As I shuffled into the barn and made my way up the ladder to the loft, I expected someone to yell at me for running off. No one did. In fact, there wasn't even anyone around. I debated grabbing my stuff and bolting right then and there, but since the lights were on in the loft and in the main house, I decided to wait.

A little rest won't hurt, I thought, eyeing the feather bed. I flopped down on my stomach and let my heavy eyelids shut out the harsh light from the bare bulb hanging from the rafters. I drifted off to sleep, travelling back in time, hearing her voice … her sweet voice …

> "Poor little Robin goes walkin,' walkin,' walkin' to Missouri, he can't afford to fly," she sang, pulling the covers up to my chin. "Got a penny for poor little Robin, walkin,' walkin,' walkin' to Missouri, got a tear drop in his eye." She kissed my eye, and her dazzling smile broke out.

"I love you, Mom," I said, giggling as her hand slowly made its way to my side to tickle me.

"I love you more," she said, tickling me all over. I squealed in laughter as I wriggled around and tried to grab her hand and stop it from attacking me. I called for my dad to come and save me, and he came running into the room with a roar, just like he would every night, jumping on the bed and tickling her.

"Get her, Dad! Get her!" I yelled excitedly, jumping up and down on my Spider-man bed, clutching my stuffed monkey.

And as usual, they turned away from each other and started ganging up on me. I giggled and squealed until I was too tired to move. Then they tucked me in again and took turns kissing my forehead.

"You comfy, honey?" Mom said, running her fingers along my cheek.

I nodded and squeezed my monkey, curious about the strange expression that was forming on her face.

"Robin, I need to tell you something…" She said, suddenly taking Dad's hand. "Mommy is—sick. Mommy might have to go away for a while…"

I jolted upright as someone clomped into the barn and up the ladder. "You… where have you been?" Israel said as he kicked off his mud-caked work boots. "Ma slaved all day in the kitchen making the perfect meal for you, and you disappeared!"

I stretched and forced my mind to return to reality, away from the painful dreams. "I wasn't hungry. Besides… you didn't miss me."

He unbuttoned his shirt angrily and threw it on the floor. "I didn't, but the people who don't see right through you did."

"What's that supposed to mean?" I spat. Who did this guy think he was? Did he think he had me figured out, analyzed, just like Eli?

"It means that I am the only one who sees you for who you

really are. An ungrateful, selfish, self-centered child." His voice was calm and strong.

The familiar burning sensation in my chest completely incapacitated any chance of being civil. I swore at him, crossing my arms across my chest, daring him…challenging him. He didn't respond. I wanted him to snap, to jump on me, to beat me up, to swear right back at me, but he said nothing. The burning inside me only became more intensified because of his silence, and I knew he was doing it on purpose. He pulled the chain hanging from the light bulb, casting the loft into darkness. I fumed as I waited for his breathing to become heavy so I could sneak away undetected into the chilly night.

As I trudged through the wheat fields carrying only my backpack, the sense of peace that I had when I was running through the airport in Denver returned. I was free. Free to—free to what? I shivered as the Canadian October air bit through my Florida shirt. I found shelter from the wind behind one of the many hay bales, dropped my backpack, and sat down.

How could they send me here? How could they swear to take care of me and then dump me in this sewer? She lied to me. She said she'd always love me, and now look at where I am. Cold and alone in this god-forsaken field. He said he'd never leave me, even when things got hard. But that was a lie too. As soon as she was gone, he left me.

I curled up into a ball and looked up at the starry sky, wondering if they could see what their son had become because of them. The hay itched at my nose, and my head started to ache from it, but I didn't care. I'd only stay for a few minutes anyway, and then I was going to continue on my way. Find a busy highway or a lake—something to end my suffering. Anything. My eyes closed. I couldn't keep them open…

"Sing it again, Mom, sing it again!"
"Poor little Robin, walkin,' walkin,' walkin' to Missouri, got a teardrop in his eye."

DOES THIS NIGHTMARE EVER END?

"Come on, kid! Up you go!" Strong, rough arms yanked me to my feet. "Hey, George! I got him!" The policeman picked up my backpack and started dragging me away from the comfort of my hay bale.

"Hey! What the—let me go!" I whined, struggling to get away from him. They had found me. I didn't know how, but they did. I seethed inside when I realized that Israel must have reported me missing. Why didn't he just let me go? He hated my guts anyway.

"Not a chance, slick. You're going back to your auntie and uncle's." The young cop grinned obnoxiously in my face and shoved me head first into his squad car with *Peace Officer* in big red letters painted on the side. "Got him, George. Let's go."

I felt my face literally catch on fire when his partner, George, turned around in the driver's seat and laughed at me. "Look at this kid, Bret! He thinks he's the cat's meow!" I banged my fists furiously on the metal grate separating us, causing him to flinch back and scowl at me. "Hey, hey now ... none of that."

"Bite me, copper." I said through clenched teeth. They mumbled to themselves quietly, ignoring me the best they could. I couldn't believe I had let myself be so careless as to fall asleep so close to where I knew they would look! I could've been miles away, and instead I was stuck in their stinking Mountie car, going back to my hell on earth.

"So you ever thought of going to the States to become real cops?" I said, trying to get their attention. "Or are you too busy sitting on your butts eating donuts to care about real police work?"

Bret whipped around with surprising rage and hit the grate with his nightstick. "Shut up, yank! You're already in deep trouble."

"Oh yeah?" My stomach jumped at the opportunity to antagonize. "Like what? What are you gonna do to me? Force a donut down my throat?"

"Shut up!" Bret yelled. George told him to calm down. I beamed at the fact I was getting to him, grating on his nerves. I loved his red face, his popping blood vessels, his bulging eyes.

I kept going. "Do you always listen to what he says, Bart? Or are you a man of your own?"

George stomped on the brake and pulled the car over to the side of the road. "Kid," he looked back at me, "if you don't shut up, you're gonna—"

"Gonna what?" I laughed. "Your girlfriend over here gonna beat me—" I didn't even get a chance to finish my sentence. Bret flung his door open and barrelled into the back seat. I heard a sickening pop as his nightstick crashed into the side of my face. It took a moment for the pain to come, but when it did … I could barely function.

"Bret! Get off of him!" George yanked him out of the back seat and shoved him away from the car. He took my throbbing face in his hands, my cheek stinging as he gingerly touched it with his fingers. "Son, look at me. For heaven's sake, Bret. You've got to control yourself! He's just a child! Eli's gonna kill you!"

I could barely see. My head ached, my eye felt like it was

about to explode, and my cheekbone felt like it had caved in. I shoved his hands away. "Get … offa me!" I heard him yell for Bret to get back in the car, but I wasn't paying attention. I was too focused on trying not to throw up all over myself from the pain. The familiar smell of the stable and the gravel dust eventually alerted me to the fact we had arrived back at Eli's place. I braced myself for the worst. The kids started running alongside the car, poking their faces in the window at me. I took my hand away from my bruised face and banged it on the dusty glass, causing them to scatter.

"Eli!" George yelled as he slammed the car door. "Hey. Good to see you." Eli extended his hand to George, and the two men spoke in hushed voices, causally glancing over at me, brooding in the back seat.

"How's your head, yank?" Bret asked, his voice dripping with forced concern.

"It's fine. You call that a hit? My grandma could whack me harder," I lied. My head was splitting, but I didn't want to give him any satisfaction. George opened my door, took my arm, and pulled me out of the car. I was still focused on Bret. "You're a sorry excuse for a cop, you beaver-loving, donut sucker!"

Bret raised his nightstick over his head only to have George grab it from him and push him back. Eli took my shoulders and ushered me behind himself. "George, keep your young deputy in line," he warned. "Robin," he said as I tried to crane my head around him. I wanted to annoy Bret as much as I could. I don't know why.

"What's a matter, Bart? Still letting your boyfriend shove you around, you mother-f—"

"Robin! Enough!" Eli yelled, cutting off my sentence. He had his hand clutched around my wrist, and he wasn't letting go. My blood raced. I couldn't decide who I wanted to hurt more, Bret or Eli. George dragged Bret back to their car and drove away. I could still hear Bret swearing at me, wishing he could get another chance to beat me into shape.

Eli pulled me into the house, yelling at Caleb and the girls to go and play somewhere else. I saw Grandpa Joe and Israel standing next to a green tractor in the field, staring at me as Eli yanked me forward by the wrist. Martha ignored me and continued to knead the dough ball on the kitchen table while Eli took me to the living room and sat me down on the floral couch. It smelled like old people. Everything in that room even looked like old people. A grandfather clock sat ticking noisily at the bottom of the rickety stairs, and my eyes darted over to the ancient portraits of men and women that sat in antique silver frames on top of an upright piano.

Eli caught me looking around as he sat down in an armchair across from me. "This house and almost everything in it has been in our family for generations. Those pictures are from 1828. That's pretty close to the year the first camera was invented."

I crossed my arms and scowled, pretending not to be interested.

He cleared his throat and took off his baseball cap, rubbing his hand over the grey stubble on his chin. "Look, Robin, we're going to have to go over some rules." The clock chimed eight tones, each one ringing unnecessarily long in my ears, just to annoy me. "I've been informed about your...recent...suicide attempt. Attempts."

My head shot up, and I looked him in the eyes. "So? What about it?"

"Well..." I almost thought I saw his eyes glisten, "we...the family...want you to know that we'd be very heartbroken if...if you tried that again and succeeded."

"Whatever," I said, leaning back on the sofa. He was just saying that so I wouldn't do it, making a whole bunch of legal issues for them to deal with when I was gone.

"Also," he continued, "I was wondering if you'd be willing to help out around the farm. Everyone has their own jobs; it's always been that way. So it's only fair if—"

"No freakin' way," I blurted out. There was no way they were turning me into a dirty, snotty farm boy like Israel. No, thank you. I still had some of my dignity. Or so I thought.

"I see." Eli had no idea how to deal with me. I could see it in his expression.

"I'm going to my room," I said, running out of the house without looking back at him. He was such a loser. Trying to get me to work for him. He could forget it.

"Robin, wait," Eli's voice called after me. I turned around in horror, his face showing determination instead of retreat. "I won't have disrespect in my house. If you're going to live here, you have to abide by my rules. I won't have any foolishness…no drugs…no—"

My hatred spewed out in my words. "*Where* am I supposed to find that *here?*"

Eli put up his hand. "Let me finish. I don't know what you're used to in Miami, but here in—"

"That's right! You don't know! You don't know anything about me!" I screamed. I saw Israel approaching, ready to take his dad's side, but I didn't care. I'd yell at him too. "You want me here, you won't let me leave, fine! But I won't like it! I won't do anything for you! I'll do what I want!"

Israel tried to say something, but Eli stopped him. He just looked at me, sadness in his eyes as I turned on my heels and stalked off to the loft.

I threw my backpack down on the dusty floor and collapsed on my bed. I missed her. I missed her so badly. Groaning, I turned over and buried my face in the feather pillow, trying to block out the pain in my stomach. She was gone and never coming back. I clawed at my chest; my shirt was choking me. The feeling that I wanted to die had never been stronger.

I laid there for hours, trying to get a grip, trying to calm down, but nightmares plagued my moments of sporadic sleep, sending me into cold sweats and panic attacks. I think Eli came into my room around noon to check on me, but I didn't want to talk to him. I had nothing to say. I slipped further and further away, my depressive state completely incapacitating me to the point of not even realizing there was someone sitting on the edge of my bed.

"Robin," Martha cooed. "Robin, honey … you can't do this to yourself."

I felt her shake my shoulders.

"Come on, you get up and come have some dinner. It's steak and potatoes. You haven't eaten since you got here!"

I didn't want to eat. I didn't want anything from her. I groaned and inched myself away from her forceful fingers.

"Now, now … none of that. You come on. Besides, we have to discuss which classes you were taking so we can get the proper books. Israel has a bit of free time, so he has time to get your schooling in. Lord knows I won't be able to teach you!"

"No," I said, trying to forget the fact that she had just said that Israel would be my schoolteacher.

"Now, homeschooling isn't so bad. You finish earlier than everyone else! What are you? Grade ten?" She continued to shake my shoulders, her already booming voice getting louder. "Up, up."

I flung my arm at her. "No! I said no! Don't you listen? I don't want to!" I couldn't see her face, but I knew I had hurt her feelings. I sat up as I heard her struggle down the ladder, her weight straining the old wooden rungs.

"You're a real jerk, you know that? She's trying to help you."

I looked over, startled to hear someone's voice, and saw Israel sitting cross-legged on his bed, writing in a notebook. I blinked a few times just to make sure I wasn't hallucinating. "I don't want her help," I said.

He snapped the notebook shut, shoved it under his pillow, and left.

I didn't want anyone's help. I didn't need it. I had been doing just fine on my own. I forced my legs to move, pain shooting through my spine. Stumbling over to his bed, I grabbed the notebook he had been writing in from under his pillow and started to read.

His name is Robin Cane. He's my second cousin. I hate him.

I paused and debated tearing the pages out. My heart burned again, but I didn't know why. I don't know what else I had expected. I kept reading.

He's from Miami, and he acts like he owns the world. He comes traipsing in here, judging us all, looking down on us when he knows we're the only family he has left. And he had the nerve to disrespect Ma and Pa after what they're doing for him. He's always angry. He lashes out in his words, his actions, and his clothing. But you know what? He hides. That's why he wears his dark makeup. He's hiding from the world. He doesn't want us to see. Good. I don't want to see. I'll convince Pa to let him go the next time he runs away. I don't want him around here, terrorizing the girls or anything else! I want him gone. I wanted him gone the moment I laid eyes on him.

I closed the notebook and shoved it back underneath Israel's pillow. I felt like I should cry, but as usual, it didn't happen. I clenched my fists instead, my knuckles turning white.

I knew none of them wanted me here. Why are they doing this? Lying to me?

I ran out of the barn and through the hay bale-littered fields I had run through the night before. If I could make it to the town, I could find him. If I could find him, I could—he could help me. I had never been hit before, and so I figured the one who had struck me so eagerly *must* be willing—*had* to be willing to finish the job.

A DESPERATE PLEA

I had no idea where I was going, or if I was even going the right way. I knew that Eli's farm was at least a couple miles from the center of the town, but it felt as if I would never find it. I ran and ran, the chilly wind biting my face, my chest aching, my legs failing, and my Converse shoes slowly untying themselves as I pushed them past their limit. Finally, a road appeared lined with tiny, cookie-cutter houses on each side with an occasional Grandma or Grandpa sitting in a rocking chair on the front porch, staring at me as I raced by. I didn't care about them, not even the ones who called out to me or offered me a frickin' cookie. I had a purpose. A desperate one.

I spotted the police car parked on the side of the street in front of the grocery store. There he was, perfectly alone without George to hold him back. This was my chance. Dirt got caught underneath my painted fingernails as I dug a rock out of the lawn I was standing next to. I felt like I was possessed as I threw the rock at the windshield, as if someone were controlling my thoughts and my actions as I went against my better judgement. That had been happening a lot lately.

The piercing sound of the smashing glass echoed through the quiet streets of the small town.

"Hey!" I yelled, kicking the passenger door with my foot. I

could hear Bret swearing as he fussed over the scalding hot coffee that he had spilled on his lap.

"Why, you little…" He threw open his door, fury coursing throughout his entire body, causing him to shake violently as he advanced on me. *What are you doing?*"

I seized up. Suddenly, I feared him. I hadn't thought my plan through. I wanted to die, yes, but I wanted it to be painless. Bret wanted to hurt me. There was no missing the look in his eyes. But like I said before, something was controlling me, despite my better judgment. "Screw you, Bart," I said as I ran around the car away from him and smashed in the driver's side window with another rock.

"Come here!" Bret growled and leapt over the hood, grabbing the back of my sweatshirt. I didn't even fight to get away. I wanted to, but I couldn't. My diseased heart had taken over my mind. It was trying to get me killed by antagonizing the one person who wanted to beat me to death. Pain shot up my spine as Bret slammed me against the car. "I was hoping to catch you, yank. We never got to finish our discussion!"

I gasped as he jabbed his nightstick into my stomach with as much force and speed as he could, and just as I thought the agonizing throb couldn't get any worse, he did it again. My suicidal heart gave up and my rational mind took over, but it was too late. I tried to slink away, but he held me fast, his arm choking me up against the car door.

"Bret! Let him go!" George threw down the grocery bag in his hand and pulled Bret away from me. My hands immediately went to my stomach as I fell to my knees. I didn't expect it to be like that. I had never been in a fistfight, never been beaten up. The pain was overwhelming, and I didn't know what to do. I blacked out.

By the time I got my sight back, I was in the back of the police car. George was driving, and Bret was having a tantrum on the side of the road, screaming about how he wanted to get his hands on me just one more time.

I couldn't take a deep breath. When I tried, my stomach muscles would constrict and my throat would close, partly from pain, mostly from the fear of the pain.

"Robin ... " George's soft voice floated to the back seat where I sat writhing. "Robin, what are you doing?"

I didn't know what to tell him. I felt like an idiot. I finally decided on my usual response. "Butt out, hoser. You don't know me," I growled as I blinked away the dizziness threatening to make me black out again. I gingerly poked the spot on my ribs that was on fire, quickly drawing my hand away as the sickening stab pulsed through my stomach again. I never wanted to run into Bret again. I avoided George's patronizing glances in the rear-view mirror as much as I could. I knew I had just done the dumbest thing in my life, and I didn't need him to tell me.

He pulled the car up to the side of the road in the middle of nowhere and got out. Waves of panic started to crash over me as he opened my car door and pulled me out to stand beside him on the desolate dirt road. "Look," he said, holding my shoulders and staring into my unwilling eyes. "What you've got going on has got to stop. Eli's a good man. You should feel honoured to be in his house. I respect him, so if you're causing him grief every night, I'm gonna have to deal with that. The next time Bret gets his hands on you, son, he's not gonna let up."

"Are you threatening me?" I said through clenched teeth.

He let me go and got back inside his car. "If that's what it takes to keep Eli unharmed and this town safe, then yes. I'm threatening you."

I kicked the car tire in anger. The roar of the engine drowned out my foul words.

"The house is just beyond that field. Have a good night," George yelled out the window as he sped away.

I cursed. I fumed. Not because I was angry, but because I was scared. Basically George was saying that if I caused trouble one more time, he'd let Bret do what he wanted to me, and because of my idiotic tantrum, he would most likely attempt to inflict maximum damage.

"Stupid, stupid, stupid!" I fussed as I trudged through the

familiar hay-baled field. What was wrong with me? My heart raced and pounded out of my chest as I ran in anger and eventually collapsed on the ground next to a scratchy bale. "Screw this … screw it all!" I yelled to no one, looking up at the quickly darkening sky and the foreboding clouds. I laid down flat on my back and shut my eyes, willing everything and everyone to go away. Willing my life away. Slowly I started to forget … to fade away … to sleep again … and dream …

"Is there a volunteer to come up to the board and do problem number four?" The teacher's monotone voice continued to disinterest me. I seriously loathed algebra, and I dreaded fifth period every single day. I sighed louder than I should have and stretched out in my seat, desperately trying to show my boredom.

"Robin!" his squeaky, nerdy voice unhappily penetrated my wandering thoughts. "Why don't you come up here and work this problem for the class?" I heard laughter. The teacher seemed to be the only one who didn't actually know me.

"Um … no thanks," I said, not trying very hard to hide my sarcasm. I looked around at my classmates for the approval I knew I had gained by being my usual difficult and hilarious self. I especially liked the looks the girls were giving me. I tried to do my best smouldering model look at them while running my fingers through my long blond hair. I laughed triumphantly as they all blushed and looked away.

"Ahem …" The nerdy teacher pushed his coke bottle glasses farther up on his shiny nose. "Mr. Cane, please come up to the board."

I crossed my arms and smiled obnoxiously. "Why don't you just show us? I don't really feel like getting up." More laughter erupted, but it quickly died out as the teacher approached my desk and leaned on it with both hands, staring directly into my face.

"Robin, I would greatly appreciate it if you would try to respect me in my class. You might think you're better than me, but you're not. Now get up to the board, or I'll fail you, right here and now." Through his ridiculously thick lenses, his eyes were dead serious. Anger rose in my throat as I shoved my chair back and stood up nosily. He was threatening me. I hated it when people threatened. The class went silent as I shuffled to the board, snatched up the chalk, and stared blankly at the simple algebra problem in front of me. I didn't have a clue what to do. I wasn't paying attention! Usually, when a stupid kid goes up to the board in class and can't figure it out, his classmates laugh at him. My classmates didn't dare laugh. I wish they would've. Them not laughing was just another manifestation of the collective pity they had on me for my mom. It was ridiculous.

I was seriously debating writing a swear word on the board where the answer was supposed to go when the classroom door opened abruptly. The principal stood there in her perfect pantsuit and nodded at the nerdy teacher, who in turn nodded back. I put down the chalk and started to head back to my seat when he put a hand on my shoulder. "Robin, can you get your bag and come out into the hall with me?" His beady eyes, which were once threatening, glinted a little. Grateful for the chance to leave my least favourite class early, I didn't hesitate or ask why. As I stepped out to where the principal was waiting, my mind started thinking of all the bad things I had done lately, and which one was the most likely reason for why I was being taken out of class. I settled on the fact that I had stolen the gym teacher's wallet. I assumed someone snitched on me.

"Robin—," the principal started.

"Yeah, yeah … I did it. So what?" As soon as I had interrupted her, I saw Marcus standing at the end of the hall with his hands in his pockets. I looked at him, then back at the principal's misty eyes, and my gut told me exactly what had happened. I walked to where my dad was standing. "Dad? Is she okay?" He said nothing to me. He just started for the front entrance. "Dad? Dad!"

"Be quiet," he whispered without even looking at my face. I knew she had died. I could hear it in his strained and distant voice. The moment I had been dreading for the past three years had finally come. My muscles seized up, my throat closed, my heart pounded, my hands shook. He ignored me. Why was he ignoring me? I was choking. I was falling to my knees ... falling through the floor, being consumed with fire ...

My own screams woke me from my nightmare. I shook violently as I tried to stand, sweat dripping down the back of my neck, memories stabbing me in the stomach, making the already existing pain worse. I couldn't see. It was pitch black as I stumbled around for what must have been hours, looking for the faint glow of the barn or the house. I was just about to give up when a new kind of fear enveloped my senses. The petrifying kind. The disabling kind. A dark shadow was moving toward me. Shuffling toward me. I couldn't breathe, I couldn't move, I couldn't think, I couldn't scream ...

THE OLD MAN

I can't remember if I tried to get away or not, but I do remember not being able to. The shadow had taken my arm and pulled me along with it, shuffling as it had done before. Part of my mind realized it was a man, an ordinary human man, not some ghost or alien, and so my fear subsided, but then the other part of my mind realized it was a stranger, forcefully taking me somewhere, and the fear returned more intensely than before. I think it was then that I tried to wrench my arm out of his claw-like fingers, but he just held on painfully tighter. I heard him grunt and mumble something as he yanked me alongside him toward a faint glow of light. My heart raced as my mind thought up the worst possible outcomes from entering this man's cabin, but as we got closer to the light, I realized that I had heard this man mumble before, and it sounded like the same thing. "Whippersnapper."

Grandpa Joe shoved me up the rickety stairs and through the dilapidated door to his cabin. I turned around to see him hanging up his cowboy hat on a peg on the wall as my eyes adjusted slowly to the faint light of the oil lamp burning. He turned to me and stared, his old eyes scrutinizing my every movement. I was still shaking slightly, but he pushed me down into an old wicker chair, promptly sitting down in one across from me. My temper started to flare up as he continued to stare but said nothing.

"What?" I said. He said nothing in response. I crossed my arms over my chest in attempt to stop the shivering. I didn't know what he wanted and I didn't care. If he wanted to stare at me all night, then fine. I'd just sit there and ignore him. As much as I didn't want to admit it, his cabin intrigued me. Everything looked straight out of a 1940s Western movie. Yellowed newspaper clippings in picture frames, whittled wooden animals, oil lamps, old kettles and pots, even an ancient wagon wheel leaning up against the wall.

A small scraping noise turned my attention back to the old man. I looked down at the tiny table that was in between us to see a chessboard being pushed in my direction. A single white pawn had been moved two spaces, and it seemed to be my turn. I looked up at him for a sign, an indication of what in the world he wanted from me, but he was staring at the board. I reached over, picked up a black pawn, and moved it two spaces, mirroring his. Nothing happened. He didn't speak, he didn't move, it didn't even sound like he was breathing. I watched him intently, curiously; my anger had been replaced by wonder. Slowly, his wrinkled hand rested on his bishop, and he slid it forward. I shoved another pawn across the squares carelessly. Before I knew it, he had beaten me. Wordlessly and without emotion. He had calmly set me up and taken every one of my pieces. I didn't care. I didn't understand. Once he had knocked over my king, he stood up and took my arm again, leading me to the door. He gently pushed me outside, turned me in the direction of the barn, and closed the door behind me, disappearing inside. I stood on his porch, gaping, amazing, confused by the old man and his chess game. What did it mean? What was he saying? Why didn't he speak? Was he just crazy?

My untied Converses flopped about as I made my way to the barn and up to the loft. I had no idea what time it was when I finally made it back to my bed. I didn't even look to see if Israel was there.

THE AWAKENING

"Earthquake!"

I lurched upward, my skin crawling, my head reeling, my eyes desperately trying to focus.

Israel was standing at the foot of my bed, his arms crossed, his jaw firmly set. "You are going to come and eat breakfast, because my mom made a feast, and she'll cry if you don't show up this time."

I tried to calm my racing nerves as I flopped back down face first into my feather pillow. "I'm not hungry," I said, which was a lie. I was starving. The last meal I had had was on the airplane, and I hadn't even eaten the entire thing.

"Don't lie to me, Miami. Get up. Come on. Pancakes. Bacon." Israel yanked the covers off me.

"Hey!" I yelled, stumbling out of bed and attempting to threaten and intimidate him—or at least show my annoyance.

He ignored my childish glares and threw my crumpled t-shirt from the floor at me. "Come on. She's waiting."

I wrenched it over my head and followed him reluctantly and as noisily as I could down the ladder and to the house. As I rubbed my dry and itchy eyes, my heart sank. My eyeliner had worn off almost completely. I almost turned and ran, but the smell of bacon and eggs overtook my senses, and it was then that

I realized exactly how famished I was. I forgot about my exposed blue eyes, but I slowed my pace as we got closer to the front door. I felt unwelcome, unwanted. I didn't want to go inside. I felt Israel's hand on my back.

"Come on," he said gruffly, pushing me forward through the screen door, down the hallway, and into the noisy kitchen. Esther and Eve looked up from their pancakes to see who had entered but quickly turned their heads to each other and started whispering, casting me frequent, frightened glances.

"Robin! Good morning," Martha said in her sickly sweet, singsong voice. "Take a seat and let's get some goodness in you!" Israel shoved me down into one of the empty chairs that just happened to be right next to Caleb. The book-reading boy didn't even glance up at me. Israel then took a seat right across from me and watched me. Probably making sure I didn't try and murder his precious little brownnosing brother.

Martha placed a huge platter in front of my nose filled with scrambled eggs, crispy bacon, two fluffy pancakes, and a bunch of grapes. My stomach pleaded for me to eat it, and I did. I shovelled it into my mouth as fast as I could. I didn't care if they were all staring. I had never been so hungry in my life. After I had finished, I leaned back in my chair and sighed. Martha was beaming at me. I looked away from her and noticed that the twins were staring at me again. I stared back and let my pupils wander in different directions—a freaky trick I had always been able to do. They hastily asked their mother if they could be excused and then ran outside. Caleb, the little bookworm, stood up and started clearing the dishes from the table. I took that as my cue to get out of there. As I scooted my chair back and started to stand up, someone shoved me back down. Israel didn't take extra care to be gentle.

"You sit tight, Miami. Ma has to go over your school with you." His hand stayed on my shoulder, pressuring me, controlling me.

Martha scowled at him. "Israel, don't be patronizing."

"Yeah, don't be patronizing," I mumbled sarcastically, shrugging his hand off me and standing up. His eyes narrowed as he crossed his arms, refusing to leave me alone with his mother.

Martha dried her hands on the dishtowel Caleb was scrubbing away with furiously and ushered me into the old-people living room. My feet were dragging as much as they could. "Now…grade ten, right? We still have those books. The girls don't get into them for another year or so." Her pudgy little fingers skirted over an overwhelming, dusty bookshelf, pulling out ancient textbooks and tossing them on the coffee table. "What are your strongest subjects?" She smiled at me and waited patiently for my answer, while Israel's eyes said, *He probably fails them all.*

And in all honesty, I had stopped trying at my schoolwork before I even reached high school. What good was school when I didn't have a future to put anything I might learn to use?

"Lunch," I said idiotically.

"Aww…" Martha cooed and approached me. "Now, now, don't be shy. I'm sure there's something you're good at!" She put her arm around my shoulder and squeezed with all her might.

My insides burned. I didn't want her to touch me. I twisted away, immediately masking my pained gasp. I moved the injured muscles in my stomach. "I'm not much for school," I said darkly, trying to inch toward the exit.

Martha didn't even notice my coldness toward her attempt at a loving gesture. "Well, most teenagers say that. But once you get into it, it'll be fun! Now, here's algebra two. Did you do algebra one?"

My nightmare came flooding back. Me, standing in front of the class, not knowing what to write on the board. My disgusting blond hair. The nerdy teacher. The principal interrupting. My dad crying. "I don't want to do algebra," I said, backing up.

"Well…" the light in her eyes was dimming at my uncooperativeness. "You kind of have to."

"No, I don't!" I said, louder than necessary. "I'm not becoming a *homeschooler.* No way. I won't. I don't want to. I don't have to." I turned on my heels and dashed out. I felt like a little child. Tantrums, "I won't!" and running away? Stupid, but I didn't know how else to respond. They were trying to change me. I didn't want to be changed. I didn't need to be changed. I wasn't going to be there much longer anyway. I wandered around the yard for a while, not knowing what I was doing. Everything felt like a really long nightmare. Not reality, but at the same time it couldn't be more real. As I passed the old man's cabin, I thought I saw him watching me out of the curtained window, but when I looked, he wasn't there. He freaked me out. Was the chess game a dream? Or did that really happen? I sat down with my back against the wooden fence that surrounded the garden.

Think, Robin. This is ridiculous. This is no life! Hiding from the world, being threatened by wannabe cops, forced to become some dumb farmer? These people hate me! Why are they keeping me here? Why can't I get away?

I watched the yellowed leaves rustle in the trees as the wind licked at them, gently tearing them off, sending them floating to the ground. This place was so different than Florida, and oh, how I longed to be back home. A stab of jealously coursed through my already aching stomach as I tried to think of who my band would've replaced me with as their drummer. My heart started its usual routine of burning me. I think I groaned aloud.

"Are you okay ... Rob—Robin?" A slightly confident but shy voice woke me from my morose state. I turned my unwilling head over my shoulder to see the redheads approaching cautiously. "It sounded like you hurt yourself." Eve's green eyes filled with compassion.

I was shocked that they were even speaking to me. "Uh ..." I had no idea what to say. They walked around the fence and stood directly in front of me, towering down. I watched them. Eve, the one who had spoken, was staring at me with wonder, apprehension, and care. The other one, Esther, was hiding behind her sister as if she were looking into the face of death itself. "I'm fine," I mumbled, not taking my eyes off them. What were they up to? Were they trying to trick me?

Eve put her hands on her hips. "You didn't *sound* fine. You sounded—"

"I'm fine!" I said angrily, standing up and skirting around them. They followed me.

"Where'd you get that bruise on your face? Pa says you're not fine. Pa says you have—"

"Eve! Stop," Esther interrupted. I was still trying to get away.

"I can talk if I want!" Eve retorted. "Robin doesn't mind me talking to him, do you, Robin?"

I let that one go unanswered. Ask a stupid question, get ... Well, she didn't even deserve a stupid answer.

"What's it like in Florida?" she pestered.

She pestered a long time. I walked and walked, speeding up, slowing down, darting here and there, ignoring her the whole way, but they followed and she talked. Finally, I gave up running and sprawled out flat on my back down in the middle of my favourite field, my two shadows sitting down right next to me. Apparently, they had taken my silence as a sign of friendship.

"Why won't you talk?" Eve whined, tucking her fiery locks behind her ears and watching me intently as I stared up at the sky.

"I don't want to talk to you," I said matter-of-factly.

"Eve, let's just go," Esther's timid voice pleaded.

"No! Robin, do you want us to leave you alone?"

Another stupid question, I thought. "What do you think?"

"We'll leave if you answer three questions."

I weighed my options. Stupid questions and silence or not talking and getting stuck with bothersome leeches for the rest of the day. "Fine. Question one."

"Okay!" I could hear the triumph in her voice. "How old are you?"

I sighed. "Sixteen," I said, closing my eyes, willing the interrogation to pass by quickly and painlessly.

"Oh my gosh, you're like ... "

Oh gosh ... oh my ... like ... like ... like ...

"You're like, two years and ... a few months older than us!"

Great. Can we please be best friends now? Please? Oh, please? "Next question," I groaned.

"Okay … um … do you have a girlfrien—"

"No," I cut her off.

"Okay…" the eagerness was quickly dissipating from her voice. "Um … what's your favourite thing to do?"

"I like to kill things that talk too much!" I blurted out.

Eve's perfect little face scrunched up in defence. "Hey! You're mean, you know that?" She stood up and pulled her trembling sister away with her. "Why are you like that? I'm just trying to be friendly!"

I didn't answer. I closed my eyes and waited for them to leave me alone. Shivering, I lay there alone for hours, moping, brooding, and trying to convince myself that things couldn't possibly get any worse. But I could never have been more wrong.

EVERYONE JUST GETS WEIRDER

I felt like there was someone watching me. I felt their eyes. I sat up and scanned the trees and the field. No one. My skin started to crawl, just like it had done the night before when Grandpa Joe had found me in the dark. I stood, ready to brace myself against the attack I was sure was imminent.

"Hello, Robin Cane," a soft, velvety, eerie voice came out of nowhere.

I wanted to panic, to race for the barn as fast as I could, but something held me rooted to the spot. My eyes continued to dart around, looking for the nonexistent voice. "What do you want?" As soon as I spoke, I saw him. Caleb. Gliding out of the trees, heading directly for me. I was expecting my fear to reside, but it increased.

"I wanted to talk to you," he said, approaching me, gazing into my eyes, scaring me to death. I think I actually stepped away from him.

"About what?" I said quietly. I had the strangest urge to respect this scrawny kid, and it enraged me. I crossed my arms. I don't know why.

His crystal blue eyes scrutinized me, and his chocolate brown hair fell into his eyes as he tilted his head to the side. "Why do you want us to hate you?" His eyes stayed completely focused on me as I fidgeted. He waited for me to answer his prodding question.

Whatever was beating in place of my heart practically stopped. "I don't really give a crap what you guys think of me, kid. Now go away." I turned from him.

"I know you care." His calm voice sent shivers down my spine. "I can see it. You don't have to hate us. We won't break your heart."

"You don't see nothing, you little brat! Now get away from me and stop analyzing!" I broke into a run, but his face and his crystal eyes were burned into my memory forever. I tried to shake it, forget his words, but there was something about him. What was he, like, ten or something? But it felt like he was just as creepy as his grandpa. I'm not usually frightened by people, and when I am, it's because they're bigger than me and they want to hurt me. But Caleb … he frightened my very core. I had never felt more confused.

As I walked through the fields and back toward the barn, I realized I knew exactly why I was afraid of him. He saw right through me. He knew exactly what was going on inside my head. He knew I was pushing everyone away; he knew I was trying to get them to hate me so I wouldn't have to worry about being hurt again. But I wouldn't stand for it. No one could know. They wouldn't understand. They would just misinterpret and then screw my life up even more.

I went back up to the loft and stood in the middle of the rickety wood floor. It had only been three days since I had arrived at my new "home," but it felt like it had been an eternity. An endless eternity of emptiness, boredom, painful dreams, and suicidal thoughts. Robotically, I walked over to my bed and sat down. What else was there to do? I lay down on my stomach and buried my bruised face in the beaten-up feather pillow I had become very fond of. I didn't want to sleep for fear of the nightmares I knew would come, but my masochistic heart took over again and slowly lured me into a deep, black sleep...

"I'll be over tonight at like, eight!" Justin yelled after me as I ran up the steps to my house.

"Don't forget your amp this time!" I responded, knowing he'd forget it anyway. I grinned; tonight was our rehearsal. Our band had just gotten a gig at another high school dance, and we wanted to make sure we were ready. I threw my bag down on the kitchen counter and yanked open the fridge, looking for something to eat. Out of the corner of my eye, I saw the calendar on the wall above the phone. Two years today. Two years ago she had died. Two long years ago, my dad had come to my classroom in the middle of the day to tell me. I knew what had happened before he had said a word, and it felt like someone had stabbed me in the gut. I think I passed out right there in the hallway, but I'm not sure. That's one of the memories my mind blocked out.

As I was looking for a snack and tugging on my newly dyed black hair, I tried to shake those memories out of my mind. Today was supposed to be happy. My band was coming over, we had a paid gig. Life was finally looking up.

I climbed the stairs two at a time, anxious to tell my dad about the gig. Maybe he'd smile at me for once. Maybe he'd finally be impressed that someone was interested in what I did. Or maybe he'd nod and ignore me as he usually did. I carefully opened the door to his office. He wasn't at his desk. "Dad?" I said softly and listened. No reply. Not one sound. I looked out the window to see if his car was in the driveway. It was. "Dad?" I called again. Still no answer. A strange feeling came over me; he was always home at this time. Always. I walked slowly to his bedroom. The door was ajar. My skin started to crawl. I tried to call out for him again, but my words caught in my throat. I pushed the door open and stood, frozen in horror at the sight of his lifeless body sprawled across the bed. My ears rang, my knees locked, my fingers went numb. My senses tried to shut out the spicy smell of blood that permeated the air...

"Miami! Dinner!"

Pain shot through my back and neck as I was yanked out of my sleep at the sound of Israel's impatient voice. Trembling, I covered my nose and mouth with my sweaty hand. I could still smell the fresh blood. I thought I had replied, I thought I had said, "I'm not hungry," but he yelled at me again for an answer and then proceeded to climb the ladder.

"Robin... let's go. *Eli* wants a word with you." His voice was straining to sound kind. "Robin? What are you doing?"

What *was* I doing? My back was pressed up against the wall, the blankets clenched in my white fists becoming damp from sweat. I forced myself to shift from my petrified state into an unstable upright position, avoiding Israel's concerned eyes. "Um..." I stammered. "I was... uh... doing nothing."

To my surprise and annoyance, he came closer and reached out to me. "Are you okay? Do you need help?"

I jerked away from him. "No, I don't need your help!" I stumbled out of bed, my feet tangling in the sheets. I didn't want his lying pity. I read his journal. I knew how he felt about me.

He put his hands up in the air. "Fine. You don't want my help, so be it. But you have to eat or you'll starve to death. So come."

"Why doesn't anyone ever let me do what I want?" I screamed. My heart pounded in my ears as I forced myself to calm down. I didn't want him to know what I was thinking. I didn't want him to hear my ranting. I didn't want him to see inside me like Caleb could. I stayed standing with my back toward him, ashamed and embarrassed that I had just had another childish outburst.

He didn't say anything. I'm pretty sure he didn't know what to say or even think. I heard him leave quietly. I turned around and rubbed at my eyes, wishing I could cry. Crying might satisfy the ache, the sting, but nothing I did made the tears come. I pulled my sweatshirt on angrily, cursing the cold weather I was not used to. I missed Florida with all my heart, and as much as I was trying to put everything I had loved behind me, I missed my friends the most. Who was I kidding? I couldn't live like this. I couldn't live hating the world. I had never wanted it to be this way! I had never made that choice. It was my decaying heart that was trying to destroy me. I couldn't let it. I'd have to destroy it first.

My feet carried me to the ladder and down into the barn below. The mud-caked hay stuck to the bottoms of my shoes as I walked and surveyed my surroundings. My eyes rested on the wooden rack in the corner of the dusty room. Two rifles and two shotguns sat in their holsters, beckoning me forward.

Just do it. Finally, there's no one to stop you. This is what you want. There's nothing for you here; no one cares about you. Do it. The pain will end. The heartache will disappear. Do it. Take it!

The voice inside my head grew louder and stronger as I approached the weapons rack. My hand flinched at the touch of the cold barrel of the shotgun. My fingers slowly curled around it, gripping it. I could feel the peace. The promise of redemption. The horror.

The barn door creaked open.

I yanked my hand away and whipped around.

Grandpa Joe approached me slowly and intently and took my arm, just as he had done before. I wanted to stay—stay and grab the gun, pull the trigger—but I let him lead me away. I shivered against the cold autumn air as he took me to his old cabin.

He shoved me down in "my" chair and pushed the familiar chessboard toward me, offering me the first turn. I stared at it. I still had a hard time figuring him out and understanding why he was doing this. Did he get some kind of pleasure from watching me lose? Did he just love to win? But then why didn't he gloat about it afterwards? Why did he stay completely silent? When I failed to make my first move within his allotted period of time, he pushed the board forward slightly. I unfolded my arms from across my chest and gave in. My hands were still stiff from clutching the cold barrel of the gun, and I felt like he could see. I moved a pawn two spaces forward and quickly folded my arms again.

We played, silently, just like before, for about an hour. He took about five minutes for each of his turns, he thought about it so hard. Meanwhile, while he was enjoying my incompetence, my stomach started to ache. Probably from lack of food. I waited, utterly bored and wiped out, as he debated whether to take my queen with his bishop or his pawn. It didn't really matter. He had won anyway. My mind wandered back to the gun resting quietly in the corner of the barn. Looking back at the wrinkly, strange, and creepy old man, I longed for the weapon to be in my grasp.

Time crawled at a crippling pace, the ticking of the clock etching every moment of my agony into my skin. Grandpa Joe slowly reached for his piece to checkmate me, but then he pulled his hand back. He did the same thing again two minutes later. The third time he drew his hand back, I had lost it.

"Just frickin' take it already! You've already won!" I snapped.

The old man looked at me; disappointment riddled his face. He moved his piece, abruptly stood, and started ushering me to the door in his usual fashion.

"I can walk! Why do you push?" I whined under my breath as I was carefully forced out the door. Man. Could these relatives get any weirder?

I clomped down the steps with the intent of going back to the barn and to the instant relief that awaited me there, but lo and behold, another one was waiting for me.

"Robin, we need to talk," Eli said, striding over, his kind face distorted with a recently familiar determined harshness. "Your behaviour is somewhat unacceptable."

I tried not to laugh in his face. "Somewhat?"

He ignored my usual sarcasm. "Martha told me you've refused schooling. You can't do that, Robin."

I sighed and tried to walk past him. He grabbed my arm.

"Do you hear what I'm saying to you?"

"No," I spewed. "You've been talking, but you haven't really been *saying* anything!" I tried to pull my arm away, but he held on as if his life depended on it.

"If you won't do your schooling here, you'll go to public

school." Eli's grip tightened as he tried to force his words to be soft. I winced.

"Fine. I don't care. I hate it here anyway." I tried to wrench away from him again, but he pulled me closer. Fear punched me in my sore stomach. "You can't treat people like this!" I yelled.

"Do you enjoy acting like a child?" he growled in my face.

I recoiled.

He let go.

"Tomorrow," he said, "Israel will walk you to school, show you where it is."

My heart raced at a million miles an hour. My arm stung where he had gripped me. I was so angry, I forgot about the guns waiting patiently for me in the barn as I stormed back to my room. Would this nightmare ever end? Martha badgering me, the girls torturing me, Caleb freaking me out, Grandpa Joe wasting my time, Eli threatening me … What else could possibly grate on my nerves?

"You feel any better?" Israel's voice carried down the ladder as I inched my way up.

I had forgotten Israel. I wondered what he would do to me. "None of your business," I mumbled, making my way to my bed, keeping my eyes away from him.

"Don't you get bored? Sitting around all day … sleeping?" Israel looked up wearily from his journal writing, his eyes tired and worn.

"No," I said curtly, pulling out my iPod and shoving my over-sized headphones on my head. He watched me. I stared right back at him. I knew what I was trying to say. *Don't mess with me. Don't talk to me.* But I had no clue what he was trying to say or what he was thinking. Finally, I relented and closed my eyes. I didn't want to spend my evening staring into the eyes of another guy. When I opened them a few minutes later, he was gone, journal sitting in the middle of his pillow. I slid my headphones down to my neck, straining to hear a sound that would tell me where he had gone. Total silence. I leaped up, grabbed the brown leather book, and flipped to the most recent entry.

I don't know what to think anymore. He's so stupid. He's so foolish and uncooperative! Doesn't he know that we chose to have him sent here? Doesn't he realize we want to love him? I'm so afraid he'll try to kill himself again. I know I said I hated him, but I really don't. I just didn't know how to respond. Now I do. He's in so much pain. I wish he would let me help him. He cries out in his sleep. I don't know what to do. It sounds like someone is hurting him, but it's just a dream. I wish I could help him, but he doesn't want me to. My hatred is gone, yes, but what has it been replaced with? Pity? Compassion? Worry? Or is it fear?

Hearing footsteps, I hastily closed the book and replaced it on his pillow. By the time he had made it up the ladder, I was lying in bed, pretending to be asleep and reminding myself to try and make sure I didn't … cry out … in the middle of the night.

WRONG CROWD

Martha handed me a red backpack and a brown paper bag. I felt like I was in a dumb, family TV drama where the kid gets ready for his first day of school, and the oversized mother sheds a tiny tear. Except in this case, I believe Martha's tear was a tear of joy. "Be good," was all she said as she headed back to the kitchen table where Caleb and the girls had their math books open, being diligent homeschoolers and all. Automatically, I shoved the stupid brown bag into the stupid red one and flung it over my shoulder.

"Let's go. We'll be late for school if we don't leave now," Israel said, twisting his Edmonton Oilers baseball cap on his head. I wanted to swear at him, to smash in his head with the dorky red backpack filled with who knew what. He was treating me like a preschooler. I stayed silent. I didn't feel like having an all-out fight. "So Dad called them and sent your papers and stuff. So everything's set."

I still stayed silent. I shivered in the cold as we walked down the gravel road toward town.

"It's going to snow eventually. You'll need warmer clothes than just a sweatshirt." Israel's patronizing tone stung my ears.

"I'll figure something out," I mumbled. I watched him as he walked slightly in front of me, looking as if he didn't have a care in the world. He pitied me. I hated it when people pitied me. The people at my dad's funeral pitied me, and so did that "monster number two" guy the government sent to take me away from my home.

We made it into town in about twenty minutes. My skin crawled as we passed the police car sitting in its usual spot outside the grocery store. My wary eyes scanned the area for Bret, my favourite "peace officer," but he was nowhere to be seen. My heart rate slowed back to normal as we turned the corner, the car out of sight. As we approached the school, I decided it had to have been the biggest building in the whole town. I was expecting a little red country schoolhouse, but this place wasn't half bad. "How many go here?" I asked Israel as he led me closer and closer to my doom.

"About two hundred fifty. All the farming communities send their kids here." Israel's voice was wistful; he obviously hated being homeschooled.

My sophomore class alone in Miami had about four thousand kids. Two Hills High School would definitely be different. I groaned inwardly. It would be just like a private school. Everyone would know everyone. Everyone would date everyone else's girlfriend or boyfriend. There would be no secrets and too many rumours.

Fine. They can send me here, but I won't like it. I refuse to become one of—these people.

"Israel, good to see you!" A tall, curly-haired man shook Israel's hand eagerly as we entered the building. "How's Eli?"

Good grief. Does every single person in this cruddy town know Eli?

"Ah, Bob ..." Israel attempted a smile while avoiding my eyes. "He's—all right. Dealing with some ... issues, but he's okay."

Yeah, why don't you just say "dealing with me"? Me: the American criminal.

"And you are Robin Crane," Bob said, extending his hand to me.

Robin Crane. Brilliant. Funny. Hilarious. I did not take his hand. "Do you think that's funny?" I said dryly.

Bob took his hand away and looked nervously at Israel.

"Cane. His last name is Cane, Bob," Israel corrected.

Bob laughed. "Oh, sorry! I got confused." His laughter faded when he realized I wasn't reciprocating his ridiculous glee. "Um...well...should we get you settled in?"

Israel nudged me with his foot. "Whatever," I said, ignoring Israel's good-bye as he headed out the door and I followed Bob down the hallway. I completely zoned out as Bob rambled on and on about my schedule, the rules, the times, lunch, and whatever else could possibly be droned on about. I snatched the paper with my schedule on it and skirted away from him as fast as I could. I was new in school, but I didn't need a babysitter. I could figure it out on my own. I looked at the first class that was listed.

Biology—Room 101, Mr. Penner

I looked around for room numbers and followed them until I reached the right room. The bell rang, and I sat in the only empty seat in the middle of the class. Sixteen pairs of eyes glued to my face. I ignored them all.

"Morning, guys. How's everyone doing?" The teacher reminded me of my old algebra teacher with the coke bottle glasses, except this guy had a nice, shiny bald head to go with the glasses.

The class responded in a cheerful way, finally turning their curious eyes away from me and resuming their own lives.

"Good, good. We have a new student joining us, if you didn't notice," he said, leaning casually against his desk. "This is Robin, everyone. Robin, would you like to introduce yourself to the class?"

"Um...not really," I said without thinking. I expected snickers. I heard nothing.

The teacher shrugged his shoulders and started to walk up and down the rows of desks. "This is Robin Cane; he's from Miami, Florida." A series of "oohs" and "ahhs" echoed throughout the room. "He's staying with the Neufeldts, and you should all go out of your way to make him feel welcome, as this place is very different from what he's used to." The teacher then approached me. "Here's the textbook for this class, Robin, and my name is Mr. Penner."

I took the heavy green and black book and let it drop noisily on my desk. "Thanks," I mumbled, trying to ignore the stares I was receiving. Mr. Penner didn't rebuke me for dropping the book, and he didn't yell at me to respect him with my words. He smiled. He turned his back to me and went back to the front of the classroom, proceeding with his lesson.

"Today, as I said, we will start learning about the different classifications of the animal kingdom. We'll start with—" he looked through his notes "—the protozoa of the Protist Kingdom! Does anyone know what that means?" A bunch of hands shot up. "Yes, Sarah?" Mr. Penner pointed at the tiny girl in the front.

"Protozoa are simple, single-celled animals, usually microscopic in size," she said airily. Her short blond hair bounced around her ears as she re-situated herself in her seat.

"That is correct," Mr. Penner said happily and then continued with his lecture. I looked around at my classmates, not giving a second thought to what he was saying about his precious *amoebas and parameciums.* Sarah, the know-it-all, was sitting in front, listening as if the Pope himself were speaking, and she was surrounded by other know-it-alls. I logged away the faces of the entire front row as people to avoid. The ones sitting in front of me and to my sides were all shapes, colors, and sizes. There was a fat kid stuffing his face discreetly with a chocolate bar, a brunette and a blonde texting on their hidden cell phones, trying not to giggle out loud, and we can't forget the sports jocks staring at them. The guy sitting right next to me with pale skin and bright red hair was typing furiously on his laptop, trying to get every single word of Mr. Penner's lecture. I rolled my eyes. There was one in every class. Besides those, every other kid was—can you guess? A typical farmer. Flannel. Checks. Jeans. Overalls. I glanced over my shoulder to see where the snoring was coming from. A dark-skinned kid was sprawled on his desk, dead asleep, curly black hair sticking out from all sides of his baseball cap. At least he had the right idea.

As Mr. Penner turned to write something on the board, I twisted around in my wooden desk seat and looked behind me. I met three pairs of black eyes. One of the boys was sitting with his feet resting on the side of the desk, headphones on and completely zoned out, but the other two were glaring at me. I glared back.

"What'chu lookin' at, bro?" one of them spat.

Mr. Penner stopped talking. "Alex, don't—"

Alex cut him off. "You looking at me, yank?"

I straightened up in my seat. I would not be bullied. "Don't flatter yourself, dude." I jumped out of my seat as he sprang over his desk faster than I could blink. I felt his hands brush my throat; Mr. Penner had stepped in between us. Alex's eyes flared with my demise.

"Alex! Sit down!" the teacher ordered. Alex's friend pulled him back into his seat. Mr. Penner took my arm and led me to the front of the class. He pulled up one of the know-it-alls and shoved me into his seat, sending the disappointed nerd to my old seat in front of the bully.

"Now … as I was saying … "

I zoned out for the last twenty minutes of the class. I could feel Alex's eyes boring a hole into the back of my skull. The bell rang. I was the first one out the door. I didn't want to get my face smashed in. Not just yet.

The rest of the day sucked. Algebra two: pop quiz, which the tyrannical teacher made me take, which I failed. As usual. I had gone through freshman year twice, failing algebra the first time and barely scraping a D the second. I don't know why I expected anything different to happen in my sophomore year. North American History: I fell asleep during the war documentary that was shown. French: I was completely lost. Do I know French? No. Do I want to know French? No. PE: Now, that was interesting. I befuddled the teacher because I refused to play volleyball. I guess no one had ever refused her before. English: Exciting, only because Alex was in that class too. He and his two goons. It was the last class of the day.

The bell would ring in two minutes. I didn't know what to do, but I would have to decide fast. I knew they were going to jump me. One minute. Should I run? Should I fight back? I looked around. A bunch of the kids were kids from biology, and they all knew my fate. They were looking back and forth at me and Alex nervously. I guess they were on my side. Ten seconds. Alex was inching toward me. I looked at the teacher to see if she would step in. She was already packing up her bag as fast as she could. Even the teacher was afraid of Alex! Five... four... three... I tightened my grip on my bag.

Now don't ask me what I was thinking. I can't answer. As soon as the shriek of the bell filled the room, I jumped up on my desk, jumped onto the desk beside me, and out of the open window (silently thanking the middle-aged teacher for having hot flashes). The surprised exclamations of the students and impressed shrieks of the girls were almost enough to make me smile as I was running for my well-being. I expected the bullies to be slow and clumsy, not like the thugs in Miami, but I was unpleasantly surprised. Especially when they caught me.

Pain exploded in my lower back as the headphone kid kneeled on me, squishing me into the cold ground. I couldn't move an inch.

"What is his name?" Alex growled. "What is your name?" he asked me. What the idiot didn't realize was that it was impossible to talk when you have a huge sack of bones and muscle sitting on your chest. When I only gasped and didn't answer, he turned to the other glaring goon. "Name!" he screamed.

"Robin," he said, pushing his long, Native American black hair back.

Alex leaned over me, snarling. "Robin... who the hell do you think you are?"

My eyes started blacking in from the sides. I was just waiting to hear the crunch from my ribs snapping in two.

"Max! Get off him! He can't talk, you idiot!" Alex shoved the guy sitting on me off my throbbing chest. I groaned as he pulled me up by my shirt collar. A crowd had formed.

Great. Now my demise will be met in an embarrassing way in front of a lot of people.

"No one makes fun of me!" Alex spat in my face.

"I haven't—," I croaked, "—the slightest idea why not. I'm sure it's not because they can't find anything."

He roared, but it almost couldn't be heard over the laughter. He raised his fist to punch me in the face, but I brought my head up under his chin before he could hit me. He groaned and stumbled back. I took my chance and ran into him headfirst, punching at anything I could get my hands on. I felt four hands grab me and try to pull me off, but Alex's strained voice yelled at them to stay back. "He's mine!" he yelled. I don't know how long we fought. The pain was almost unbearable, but whatever was driving me didn't seem to care. My eye exploded in pain as his fist connected with it, but I'm sure he felt the same when my elbow smashed into his cheek. All of a sudden, nothing hurt anymore. I was lying flat on my back, panting heavily. I looked to my side. He was doing the exact same thing. I struggled to stand, trying to control my panic as I wiped a ton of blood from my mouth. "Loser," I mumbled. I didn't mean to say it out loud.

Alex leaned up on his elbow, a smile inching out of the corners of his mouth. He laughed, to my surprise, and extended his hand to me as he stood up. "I have to admit, dude ... that's never happened before."

I took his hand. At least I wouldn't have to worry about being mauled every day at school.

"This is Max and River." He pointed to the big headphone guy and then to the guy with long black hair. They both mumbled their hellos but continued to watch me warily. "Welcome to Alberta," Alex said, his black eyes narrowing. I knew he was bad news. These were the kind of people Justin had kept me away from in school.

"Whatever," I said, walking away, the crowd dispersing.

They followed me. "Wanna go somewhere?"

"No." I tried to avoid his convincing eyes.

"Your choice. See you tomorrow."

As I reoriented myself and headed back to the farm, the pain came back in a rush. I felt my bruised ribs from where Bret had jabbed his nightstick into my side. They hurt worse than ever. My lip was swelling, I still tasted blood, and my knuckles were completely torn up and throbbing. Yeah. So I never wanted to be in a fight again. I never wanted to go to school again. I decided to see what would happen if I refused to go.

"What happened to your face?" Eve squeaked as I walked in the front door.

I threw the ridiculous backpack down on the floor and plopped into "my" chair at the dinner table, the entire family staring at me. "What does it look like? A couple guys jumped me."

"Who?" Israel barked, but Eli held up his hand to silence him.

I lowered my battered face to my bowl of stew. I didn't want them involved in this. I could take care of myself.

Eli cleared his throat and prayed for the meal, but I could still feel eyes on me. "So other than that, Robin, how was school?"

I looked up at Eli in disbelief. How could he ask me that? "I'm not going back if that's what you mean," I said, taking huge mouthfuls of the delicious stew.

"What do you—," Israel started, but only to be stopped once more by Eli's hand.

"Robin, you have to go back to school. Everyone goes to school." Eli's voice was strained. I really *was* taking a toll on this old man.

I shook my head, pain surging through my temples. "No. I'm not going back."

Dead silence.

"Kids, can you go to your rooms please?" Eli said to Caleb and the girls. They groaned, picked up their bowls and spoons, and left me alone in the room with Eli, Martha, and Israel. My insides tightened, and the embers in my heart started to light up, ready to burn me and anyone who came close.

"Robin," Eli said harshly, "this cannot continue."

"What?" I replied stupidly. I knew what he was talking about. I crossed my arms and raised my eyebrows at him.

"This—disrespect! This refusal to do anything!" Eli's kind face was turning red and void of sympathy and patience. Martha put a hand on his arm to calm him down. "Well?" Eli yelled again.

I didn't know what to say. He hadn't exactly asked me a question. "Well what?" Shrugging my shoulders, I played the innocent victim. That did not go over well.

It was Martha who spoke up next. "Robin, it's just that ... to live in this house, you need to abide by some rules. It's just the way it's done. If you respect us, we'll respect you."

"That's a lie!" I roared. "You don't respect me! You don't want anything to do with me!" My heart had finally caught fire, and it wasn't slow in spreading.

"Now look here, you little s—"

"Israel!"

"Look here!" Israel avoided the word I knew he was aching to use and continued to yell at me. "This is ridiculous! Why can't you just try to make this work? We're trying! Why can't you? It's not that hard!"

This is definitely where I would've cried if I could have—looking at their angry faces. Their disappointed faces. Their ... fed up faces. "I don't want to make this work! I don't want to be here! I hate you guys!" I screamed, pushing my chair away from the table angrily and standing up. "Why do you even keep me here? I know you hate me too!" I stood, panting, sweating.

"Well, maybe you *should* leave!" Eli yelled louder than me and stalked out of the room, Martha at his heels. I wanted to leave, but Israel ordered me to stay. I was too exhausted to argue anymore, so I fell back into my chair without another word. He looked at me. I knew what he was thinking. He was thinking how much his life would be easier without me. How much he wanted to punch me in the face. I looked away. I couldn't take it anymore.

Eli and Martha were arguing in the other room. I could hear them. The whole house probably heard them. I sat and listened; Israel did too.

"I've had it, Martha! I can't take it anymore!"

"Eli, please ... he's our family! Our own flesh and blood!"

"No! He's unmanageable! I'm calling social services."

"No! Give him another chance! He's just a boy. Just a boy who's hurting."

"I don't know what to do, Martha ... nothing I do ... I can't ..."

"God will give you strength, Eli."

"No ... no ... this is not how I want my children to be raised!"

I knew it. I shook my head and slammed my fist on the table. I knew it! They hated me and wanted me gone. I flinched a little as Israel suddenly sprang from the table and went into the room where his mother and father were arguing. I listened.

"Dad, don't do this."

"Now you want him to stay too? I thought you of all people would want him out of here!"

"Eli, please ..."

"Dad, there are still options. Come on. We can't give up on him. If we do, then everything he's accusing us of will be true."

"Eli, Israel is right, and you know it! Shame on you! Shame for giving up, for not trusting in the Lord to bring us through this."

There was a long moment of silence between the three of them before Eli spoke again.

"I'm sorry. You're both right. I'm sorry. Lord Jesus, forgive me."

"Dad, what about Patrick? Patrick can help him. We can take him on Sunday."

My skin prickled. Who was Patrick? Some kind of torture artist? The three of them came back in the room where I was, and I had no idea how to react. Eli wanted me gone, but Israel had convinced him to let me stay. It didn't make sense, and I couldn't understand. I don't know if I even wanted to understand.

"Robin," Eli said, the kindness returning in his gentle eyes. "I'm sorry for yelling at you. But whether you understand this or not, you cannot be running around wild and doing whatever you want. We're taking you to get some help. This is your last chance."

I stood up and walked out into the frigid evening air. They were sending me to a shrink. They thought I was crazy. Maybe I was crazy.

SCHOOL OR THERAPY? SCHOOL

"Robin, this is Patrick Friesen. He's the youth leader here at church."

I looked harshly at the man that Eli was introducing me to. I wanted him to know he would never push me around. I stuck out my hand, assuming these people would think that was the polite thing to do.

"Hey, Rob. Nice to meet you," Patrick said, smiling. He was a big guy. Huge. Chunky. He was like a football player, the kind of person that almost crushed the bones in your fingers from their handshake and didn't even realize it.

"Don't call me Rob," I said dryly, trying once again to ignore the constant staring those people seemed to do! But this time, instead of angry, immature, judgmental kids, it was angry, annoyed, judgmental adults. The church folk. The Christians. They hated my guts. I could see it in their eyes. Weren't these people supposed to be loving and accepting? These ones looked at me as if I were a bug that needed immediate squashing.

I had just sat through an hour and a half of old hymns sung out of tune, the Bible being shoved down my throat, and back pain from the ridiculously uncomfortable pews irritating my bumps and bruises. Plus, I had to sit between Israel and Eli. You cannot even begin to imagine how awkward it was. I nodded off so many times, and each time I either got elbowed in the ribs by Israel, or Eli cleared his throat *really* loud. I hated it. And then, here's the clincher: they were making me meet with the youth counsellor. There he was, huge and intimidating, watching me.

"Sorry... Robin. So, Eli, how do you want to do this?" His deep voice boomed across the sanctuary. I cringed as more people turned to see what he was talking about.

"Well, I can send Israel over in the truck in a couple hours... pick him up." Eli tugged at his loosely tied tie, his unusual, un-preferred attire.

"All right then. Shall we, Robin?" He put his hand on my shoulder. Naturally, I would've shaken it off, but I didn't think I would be able to. He led me outside of the tiny church and to his black truck. We drove a short distance to the middle of the town. He lived in one of the cookie-cutter houses next to the barbershop. I knew I had to have a game plan. I couldn't let him control me. I didn't need him to tell me how to behave or how screwed up I was. I already knew I was too far gone.

"Have a seat," he said, pointing to a plush brown armchair in his living room. "Do you want a pop or something?"

I shook my head. I had decided to remain silent and now was as good a time as any to start. He sat down across from me with a big thump. I could swear the floor shook. He waited. I hated it! What was with people and staring? Did they not have any manners? I looked away from him and put my hands behind my head, determined to win.

"So how do you get your hair to do that? I tried bunches of times, but it never worked."

I tried to hide my shock and disbelief as he asked me about my hair. Like a normal person. "Uh..." So much for hiding the shock. "Um... hair glue. Backcombing." I gestured making spikes with my hands, and he smiled and ruffled his own shaggy hair.

"Yeah, I guess my hair just isn't thick enough. Weird, huh? The only part of me that isn't thick," he said.

I decided that sometime, in the far future, perhaps, maybe, I might like this guy.

"So, why black? I see you are actually blond. Why do you dress like that?"

Yeah, no. I would never like him. *What* was wrong with how I dressed? How did he know I was blond? The familiar surge of panic coursed through my body as I realized my blond roots must've been poking through.

He put his hands up in defence as he saw my unimpressed expression. "Sorry, I take it back. That's not what I meant to say. What I meant to say was why do you prefer black hair to your own?"

Because my blond hair made my Dad sick, you idiot, I wanted to shout. I didn't. "I dunno."

Patrick shrugged his shoulders. "I dyed my hair green once for a school party. It didn't work very well though."

I didn't respond.

"So how do you like Eli's place?"

"Look," I said, sitting on the edge of the armchair. "Don't play mind games, okay? I'm not stupid. I know what you're trying to do. Just—if you have something to say, just say it. I'm sick of this 'beating around the bush.'"

A small smile twitched at the corners of his mouth. Was he trying to make me angry?

"Dude… I appreciate your honesty. So hey, man, I'm gonna be honest with you." Patrick leaned forward, and the floorboards creaked. "You gotta work out some kind of compromise with your aunt and uncle. You can't just refuse to do everything and then expect to be taken care of."

I knew he was right, but it still made me feel sick. "What kind of compromise?"

He leaned back in his chair. "Go to school, bro."

My anger flared. I had almost had enough. Did anyone ever stop to think about me? How I might be feeling about this whole "relocate to a different planet" thing? All they cared about was rules and what was best for them.

"Dude, if you go to school, I bet Eli won't make you go to therapy."

My head shot up. "What—isn't this the therapy he promised?"

Patrick shook his head. "Nope. He was hoping I could convince you to go to school before he took you to a real head-shrinker."

What was the lesser of two evils? Going to school and getting pummelled and/or bothered by thugs, or having my very own psychologist to screw with my mind and make me take Ritalin. "Fine..." I mumbled. "I'll go back to school. Hopefully this means I won't have to see you again either."

He just smiled. He was so unlike all the patronizing adults I had met in the last few weeks. Let me make this clear to you though. I *didn't* like him; it was just a nice change from the harsh words I usually received.

He tried to get me to talk about my parents. That was a lost cause. He had just given up trying when I heard Israel honking the horn outside. We said our good-byes, and I got into the truck without looking back at him.

"Did you have fun?" Israel asked, his eyes on the road.

"No."

He tried to hide his annoyance. I don't even know why he bothered.

Clearing his throat, he looked over at me. "I was just trying..." He fell silent and looked away.

What was this? What was he doing? "Trying to...?" I prompted.

"I just thought... that maybe Dad would be... more... willing to try again... if you changed your mind about school."

I stopped to think. Israel's suggestion of me going to see Patrick had been the only thing that kept Eli from kicking me out. Israel wanted me to stay.

"Uh... yeah. Thanks." The sound of my voice saying thanks was the weirdest thing. I couldn't remember the last time I had been thankful for anything anyone did for me. And I guess I was thankful. I didn't want to live on the street, even if it meant sticking with the creepy, Amish farmers.

"You're welcome, Robin." His eyes locked with mine as he turned onto the gravel driveway.

I almost started to tremble. I looked away. That was how my mother had looked at me. With kindness. With care. With love.

FROZEN WASTED-ED LAND

I tugged on my scratchy woollen scarf as the biting snow tried to sneak under my collar. I trudged to school in my glorious second-hand boots, silently wishing that I would freeze to death before I got there. It had been about three weeks since I had arrived in Podunk, Alberta. It had been about four weeks since I walked into my dad's bedroom and saw him lying in a crumpled, bloody mass. It had been about one hundred and eight weeks since mom had died and left me on this planet to rot. Yes. I had been counting, and yes, I am still counting. Not one of those long weeks contained a good day either.

I stopped and looked around at the wonder of frozen rain. I had never seen it before. When it had first come down in the beginning of November, I swear I stood at my window for half an hour just watching it. It was ... beautiful; the one thing in my life that didn't hurt. The one thing I could think about without wanting to curl up in a ball and die. It was perfect, and every piece was different: cold, frozen, and delicate, ready to melt at any second. I wished I could melt away.

Things had calmed down some once I gave in and started going to school. Martha didn't cry every time she looked at me. Eli didn't look so worn out, and Israel would smile at me every once and a while. I never smiled back. I didn't know what he was playing at. When I had first arrived, I could just feel him chafing at my presence, but now it seemed as if he wanted to be around me. I tried my best to be horrid to him; maybe then he'd leave me alone. Esther and Eve of course had increased their annoying chatter because I was going to public high school, and they wanted to know all about it, especially if there were any cute boys. I just found a happy place in my mind once they started after me. Grandpa Joe had dragged me into his "cabin of torture" a couple more times to beat me mercilessly at his favourite game. The last time I was there, it looked as if he were going to say something to me but then decided otherwise. He probably just forgot what he wanted to say. I assumed he had no idea what was going on half of the time anyway. Unlike Caleb, who seemed to know everything all the time. He was always *looking* at me! Looking *through* me. I hated it! His perfect little face and perfect little voice haunted my already tormented dreams. I'll never forget the "special moment" we'd had together a few days before ...

I was just leaving Grandpa Joe's cabin when Caleb stopped me out front. He looked like a fat little snowman all bundled up in his oversized coat and hat.

"Hi, Robin," his pearly voice sang.

"Yeah, whatever," I said. My usual response to everything. I walked right past him toward the warm glow of my barn, and then he said something that almost gave me a heart attack.

"What would you say if I told you that someone died for you?"

I clutched my sweatshirt-clad arms and shivered. What did he just say? Died for me? "I don't know what you're talking about, kid."

He walked around me, slowly because of the deep snow, and stood right in my face. Or rather, under my chin, since he was so tiny. "Someone died in your place. What do you think about that?"

I knew exactly what I thought about that. "I think that's stupid," I said matter-of-factly. Why would someone die for me? What would the point be of that? I started to lose the feeling in my feet. I didn't have a chance to put my coat on when Grandpa Joe came for me, and now I was paying for it, being stuck outside with the nosey little do-gooder. I started to move toward the barn again.

"Why do you think it's stupid? Do you know who I'm talking about?" he continued, his small voice fading a little with the increasing wind.

"I have no clue who you are talking about."

Seeing as how that would never happen. No real person in their right mind would die for a lost cause like me.

"I'm talking about Jesus," he said. I felt his small, mitten-clad hand grab my scarf to try to hold me from entering the barn.

"Oh, of course! Obviously, and Santa Claus just gave me a million dollars!" My sarcastic voice carried over the blankets of snow and across the yard. I wondered if everyone heard me. I hoped they did. I looked at Caleb one last time before shutting the barn door. I shouldn't have.

"Have you ever had anyone willing to die for you because they loved you so much, Robin?" His glistening eyes widened at the wretched look on my face.

"No, but I've had someone *let* themselves die because they didn't love me enough, *and* I've had someone die because they hated me too much!" I slammed the door in his shocked little face. My blood raced through my veins, aching to go faster. My trembling hands found their way to my throat. I wanted the pain to go away, the choking to end. Why did everyone have to keep reminding me of my rejection? I knew no one loved me. I knew they had left. Why did they have to rub it in? Again, I longed for the tears to come and relieve me of my anguish, but they stayed hidden inside.

The days after that little encounter had been agonizing. My nightmares were re-runs. I had actually gotten my hands on one of those shotguns in the barn again, but I was too chicken to pull the trigger. Thank goodness for backup plans.

I got to school and shook the snow off my boots as I stepped inside the hallway, forcing the painful memories of the past days out of my mind. Most of the other kids took their coats and scarves off, but I was too cold. I kept mine on usually all day. I'm from Florida. Give me a break.

"Hey, Robin...how are you?"

I turned around at the sound of a girl's voice. "Uh...fine."

She inched closer to me, unbuttoning her red, fur-lined coat, two other Barbies at her sides. "That's good. So...we were wondering...if you were going to the Christmas Banquet with anyone?"

I stood rooted to the spot as the three girls surrounded me and kept me from leaving. The one who was speaking was the closest to my face, about three inches away, her layered brown hair falling loosely around her heart-shaped face. "Uh..." I said again. "No."

Her emerald eyes lit up. "Great! You can come with us."

No. Nope. No way. Forget it. Never in a million years. I'd rather die.

"Whatever," my pitiful self said, not realizing that they would think that meant yes.

They all squealed and clapped their hands together. "Excellent. We'll be in contact with you about our dress colors and all. See you later, Robbie," the girl with the emerald eyes gushed. They flipped their hair in unison and strutted down the hallway.

I started to yell after them that I didn't mean yes, but they were too far away, so I didn't bother. What did it matter? They'd figure it out when I wouldn't come back to school. When they heard I was dead.

Why would they even want to go with a loser like me anyway? I mean look at me! I'm a walking tragedy. A diseased soul.

I shuffled into biology, avoided Mr. Penner's insightful eyes, and plopped into the seat in the far back corner. My mind wandered back to the "special moment" with Caleb as the teacher gave us the rules for the test we were about to take. I tried to think who this Jesus character was. Something to do with the God everyone kept talking about. The God of those goody-two shoes kids at school or the neighbours at the funeral. Jesus was his prophet that lived long ago. A good teacher. Whoever. What did I know about him? Did he even exist? Did this God even exist? Apparently, he saved people. He didn't save my mom. He didn't save my dad. He wasn't saving me.

The sound of crinkling papers thrust me back into reality. Mr. Penner was handing out the tests. Alex, who was sitting in front of me this time, turned to look at me. "After school," he mouthed. I nodded, turning my attention to the three-page test I didn't care about.

Write the names of ten out of the fourteen classification groups in the animal kingdom.

I had no idea. I never paid attention in biology. I didn't pay attention in any class. The school had called Eli and Martha at least three times to inform them of my "lack of study skills," and that I was failing miserably. I didn't know what to say. I had never really been that good of a student, and nothing was about to change. I was failing three courses. I think I might have muttered "sorry" as an attempt to appease their frustration with me. But I figured I might as well give the test a try, seeing as how it was my last one. I hastily scribbled down the few things that came to my mind.

crustaceans, mammals, bugs, birds, fish, rodents,

That was all I could think of. I was impressed with myself that I could actually spell *crustaceans,* but I needed four more answers.

girls, canadians, mounties, your mom

I looked at the next question and promptly threw my pencil

down. I couldn't do it. I took a mental nap until the bell rang. I threw the paper down on Mr. Penner's desk as I walked by. He sighed at the sight of my blank answers. I didn't care.

The rest of the day consisted of sleeping through as many classes as possible, trying not to think about Caleb and his Jesus, and trying to have patience while waiting for the end of the day to meet with Alex. Now that was something that definitely weirded me out. After the first day when we had it out with each other, it was like he had a roller coaster of feelings toward me. Some days, he wanted me to hang out with him and his little gang, and then other days, he shoved me into lockers and called me names. I didn't really care what he did to me, but what I did care about was what he could do *for* me. I don't remember where I heard it or whom I heard it from, but I knew he was the guy to go to. That's why I was meeting him after school.

"Yo, bird boy!"

I turned around, almost knee deep in snow, in the parking lot where I had been waiting for fifteen minutes to see Alex, Max, and River striding up to me. "It's about time. I'm freezing my—"

"Yeah, yeah," Alex said, waving his hand in front of my face. "Whatever. You want it or what?"

My eyes darted down to the small brown package being tightly gripped in Max's hand. I nodded.

Alex looked around for anyone who might be spying on us. "We have to discuss payment," he whispered.

My teeth started to chatter. "I … don't have any money." I dug my hands deeper into my pockets.

Alex looked at Max. "Yeah, we figured. It's fine. There's something we need done." They whispered and argued with each other for a good five minutes. I tried to keep my feet moving so they wouldn't freeze off. Curse Alberta weather.

"All right," Alex said after a long debate with his evil sidekicks. "Yesterday, some of the guys from the senior class pinched most of our … stash. We have to get them back."

I stiffened my shoulders. Their pain for my relief? No contest. "Just tell me what to do."

MOMENTS OF INSANITY

I felt it morphing, evolving into a vampire-like essence, ready to strike and destroy the life of anything it got its hands on. My monstrous heart roared as I held the baseball bat over my head, ready to crash it down on one of its unsuspecting victims. There were two of them, and I had to take them out if I was to get my relief. That was fine. I could deal with that. I don't even remember doing it. One moment I was standing behind them, then the next—over them, arms aching from swinging. They groaned and turned to look at their attacker.

"What the—who are you?" was what one of them croaked out; blood running down his chin.

"He's that emo kid from Miami," the other one said angrily, getting up and starting after me. I smashed him in the face again. I heard the laughter of Alex and Max stop abruptly. I wish I would've taken that as my cue to get the heck out of there before my body fell to the ground, my face shoved into the snow.

"You have no idea how much I've been looking forward to this moment," a muffled voice said as I was being ground deeper into the freezing snow. I tried to lift my head so I could breathe, but his knee was on my neck. Snow filled my nose and mouth; I squeezed my eyes shut and tried to free myself. Suddenly the weight was gone. I sat up, sputtering and coughing, looking around to see who had pulled him off me. Alex and Max ran off in the other direction, but not before Max tossed me the little brown package, laughing. Bret chased them for a few moments, cursing as loud as he could, before he turned his attention back to me. I stuffed the package down my pants as the two seniors I had beat up scampered away.

He grabbed my arm and twisted it behind me, fire ripping through my shoulder and down my back. "Get the f—," I started.

He cuffed me on the side of the head. It was like an atomic blast going off right next to my ear. I think I cried out in pain, but if I did, I couldn't hear it.

"Watch your language, kid! I am an officer of the law!" Bret shoved me toward the parking lot. "George, I'm taking him in this time."

I looked around in a daze for George. He followed us, a safe distance behind. He wasn't going to help me this time. The ringing in my ear from Bret's angry fist tried to black out my vision as I was herded to the familiar police car. He was just about to shove me in the back when George stepped in. "Wait, Bret. Let me handle this."

Bret whipped around, still holding my arm painfully against my back. "What? Boss ... no. I got this."

George separated me from Bret's death grip. "Bret, you're too personally involved with this kid to see clearly. Obviously he was put up to this by Alex and his groupies."

The feeling in my arm started to come back, but unfortunately, that meant that I could feel George's fingers digging down to my bone. I shied away from Bret's evil eyes, wanting to kill me, not understanding why George wouldn't let him ... again. He kicked the car tires and stalked away.

"Robin..." George turned me toward him. "If anything like this *ever* happens again, I will let Bret arrest you. Do you understand?"

"That's what you said last time!" I yelled, trying to get away.

His eyes and his grip hardened. "I didn't think you would be so stupid as to pull something like this!"

My arm felt like someone had been sawing on it. "Let me go!"

To my surprise, he actually let go of my arm. "I promised Eli that I would—"

"I don't give a crap about what you promised Eli! Gosh, what are you trying to be anyway? My saviour? Why don't you just do your job? Stupid *Peace* Officer." Arm throbbing, I picked up my bag and started making my way through the snow.

"No, I'm not trying to be your saviour, Robin. But you do need one." His voice faded in the distance as I put as much space as I could between him and me. Why had he given me so many breaks? In Miami, the cops would book you for smoking a joint. Here, I had trashed their car, run away, mouthed off multiple times to the short-tempered Mountie-deputy, and beat up a couple of guys. George kept letting me go free. Why?

I rubbed my ear where Bret had hit me. It still rang. I couldn't hear very well. I pulled out the tiny brown package from my pants and stared at it in my hand. This was it. My relief. My salvation. George said I needed a saviour; here it was. I unwrapped it and stared at the bottle. Xanax. I had seen it before. My dad had been taking it when my mom was sick. It was supposed to control his anxiety. Yeah. It *really* worked. I popped open the cap and shook a couple of the little powdery white pills into my red, numb palm. They were so small. So innocent. I didn't know how many it would take. I shoved them back inside and popped the cap into place. I would figure that out when I was alone.

By the time I had reached the farm, I was practically frozen solid. I hated Canadian winters. Remember when I cursed Alberta weather? Curse it again. Suddenly, something had interrupted my cursing. Something had hit me. I turned around. "What the—"

Smack.

A ball of stinging, wet snow hit me right in the mouth. As if I hadn't had enough snow in my mouth that day. I wiped it off with the snow-coated sleeve of my coat, not accomplishing much. "Who threw that?" I growled.

Esther and Eve took off screaming. As *if* I would follow.

"Hey, Robin, sorry about that. They're just having fun." Caleb smiled at me through his thick, purple, woollen scarf and matching—what did they call it? Oh yeah. Tuque. He trudged over to me, knee deep in snow. "How was your day?"

I turned my back on him and headed for the main house. Maybe he would go away if I ignored him. Yeah, and maybe I'd grow wings and fly away.

"So did you learn anything fun?" His little voice floated behind me.

It was as if I were a little kid in kindergarten and my big brother was asking me about my day, what snack I might have had, or how long of a nap I took.

"I beat the tar out of two seniors today," I said stoically. I wanted to scare him away, but he just said nothing and followed me inside the house. My body didn't catch on to the fact that I was no longer in negative forty degrees, so it kept attempting to heat me up. My face turned beet red, and my skin felt like it was on fire. I made my way to the fridge and found what I had my heart set on, a bottle of Coke. I'll explain in a moment.

"So have you thought about what I said the other day?"

I sighed and shoved open the front door with my foot, thrusting myself into the cold air once more and heading for my barn as fast as I could. Fortunately, the little guy couldn't keep up with me. I started peeling off my layers as soon as I got up the ladder. Placing the small bottle of drugs on the nightstand, I looked around the room, just checking that there was no sign of Israel. Slowly, I pulled out the bottle of Coke and broke the seal. My heart pounded out of my throat as I dropped the pills into the dark, fizzing liquid one at a time. It had to work. I had to make sure. I put them all in, watching them each dissolve as they floated gracefully to the bottom. I must've stared at it for half an hour, sitting on the bed as the light from outside slowly dimmed. My hands shook violently as I raised the bottle to my lips, ready and willing to finally end my suffering. I hesitated. My heart was screaming for me to drink, my mind was telling me to stop, and my eyes caught a glimpse of something familiar on the floor. Israel's journal. I took the bottle away from my mouth and snatched the book off the ground.

I'll just read the last entry, and then I'll drink it. I'm just curious. No harm in being curious. I might as well indulge myself before I die.

> There was a moment where Dad wanted him out of the house, but I convinced him to let him stay. We're his only family! I can't just let him go and rot somewhere in a foster home or an orphanage, just waiting to get relocated to a prison or something. As much as he struggles and resists us, I want him here. I care about him. I want him to live…

I realized I couldn't read anymore. The book was shaking. I was shaking. I think it was my body's attempt at crying without the tears. He wanted me there? I couldn't believe it. He hated me, scorned me. Now his own words said he cared about me.

I flung the journal across the room, screaming. I kicked at anything that was within reach.

"Why am I here?" I yelled. Flashes from the past year raced in front of my eyes, jarring my senses, hitting my nerves. Everything had gone wrong. Everything had gone down the drain. I had finally figured it out. I wasn't worth anything, and no one loved me. I knew that. I accepted it. I was going to deal with it, and then Israel changed it all with his four little words: *I care about him.* Just saying the words over again in my head made my stomach lurch.

I yanked on my gritty, gel-caked hair and pounded on my forehead with my fist. Was I delusional to think that killing myself would solve anything? Marcus killed himself, and it had only made things worse. Was I being selfish? Me—my life—I—myself. Nothing was fair for *me.* But then again, who else was there but *me?* I was alone. I had been alone for a very long time.

There was no one else to think about, so why shouldn't I have the right to end *my* suffering if I wanted?

My decayed heart and soul fought with my belligerent mind for what seemed like hours, each one trying to take over the other. I couldn't come to a decision. I pounded on the walls, drawing blood from my knuckles, wooden splinters digging under my skin. My tormented eyes rested on the lethal Coke bottle diluted with drugs. Impulsively, I twisted on the cap, pushed the window open, and chucked it out into the snow. My heart raced after it, but my mind made me stay put. I had figured out the reason I couldn't go through with it. I was afraid of death. I couldn't do it. I had tried three times and failed. I was nothing *but* a complete failure. Flinging myself onto my bed, I controlled the urge to throw up. Everything hurt. My ears, my ribs, my stomach, my head, my bleeding fingers … I wanted to die, but I couldn't. The one thing that I had wanted to be entirely up to me was in its entirety, up to me—but in the end, it didn't seem as if were up to me at all.

I fell asleep hating the world. Hating my mom and my dad for dying, Israel for writing that he cared for me, Caleb for telling me Jesus died for me, and everyone else I could think of for anything I could imagine. But most of all, I fell asleep hating myself for who I had become.

IT SHOULD HAVE BEEN ME

So I'm assuming you know what it's like to wake up screaming from your own nightmare. I'm sure I've mentioned it more than once. But you know what's worse? Waking up to someone else screaming.

My eyes opened. My breathing froze. What was that? I pushed myself up and rested on my forearms, listening intently to every sound until it pierced the air once more. A bone-chilling scream. I jumped up out of my bed and raced to the tiny window that was still open. I didn't understand what I saw: a small, still, purple bundle lying in the snow, cradled in Martha's arms. In the dusky glow of the evening, I narrowed my eyes to try to make out the faces of those who were running toward the scene. Eli arrived within seconds, spraying snow everywhere as he slid to a stop beside his hysterical wife. Grandpa Joe arrived breathless not long after but soon held Eve and Esther at arm's length from their mother and father. What was in the snow?

"Caleb! Honey! Caleb, breathe! Eli, what's wrong with him?" Martha cried.

My mind slowly started to put the pieces together. Caleb: the bundle of purple. Why wasn't he breathing? A wave of realization and guilt hit me like a car slamming into my chest. The

Coke bottle. I tore myself from the window and slammed into the wall, gasping my pain and anger.

It was supposed to be me! Why did I throw it away? If I would've had the courage to finish what I started ... he would be okay.

I should've yelled to them. I should've told them what was wrong with him, but I was afraid. I forced myself to return to the window and look out at the result of my horrible mistake.

"Dad, stay with the girls!" Eli yelled to Grandpa Joe, lifting Caleb into the truck that Israel had brought to the back of the house. They sped away, tires sliding, spraying soft flakes of snow over the impressions of frantic parents and a dying child. Grandpa Joe stood, holding the confused, wailing sisters. His eyes turned on me.

I fell back from the window and covered my face in my hands. He knew. He knew what I had done. I had killed a little boy.

You didn't do what I told you. This is what happens. You failed at taking your own life, so now someone else will take it for you.

My heart tormented me with my own words. I knew they'd kill me for what I had done to their son. The bodyguard back in Miami told me this would happen. He told me I'd ruin other people's lives. I had just caused the death of a little boy by just being who I was. This was my punishment for being slow ... for being unsure ... for being alive.

I waited, pacing for hours until I couldn't take it anymore. I half climbed half fell down the ladder and stumbled in the darkness toward the weapons rack in the corner. My hands gripped the cold barrel and stock and lifted the gun off the decaying wooden frame. My whole body trembled in fear as I cocked it and held it under my chin, almost dropping it for my sweaty palms. I had finally decided. Nothing would stop me this time.

I whimpered out loud and put my finger on the trigger, ready to end it all and fix everything. Blood squirted from my tongue as I bit down on it, tense, completely drowning in terror. I choked. I gagged. But I didn't remove the gun from its place. I shut my eyes and squeezed the trigger.

Click.

My body jumped, and every muscle was wrenched in the wrong direction. I dropped the unloaded gun. It landed with a thud at my feet, just as empty as it had been when I had picked it up. My unsteady hands tore at my hair and my clothes; my voice made dark, low moans. Collapsing to the muddy, hay-covered floor, I tried to realize what had just happened. For the first time, I had actually done everything in my power to kill myself, and it didn't work. The times people said I tried committing suicide? That was just it. I had *tried* and chickened out. This time, I had pulled the trigger. I had slapped death in the face and survived.

I stayed on the cold floor of the barn for the rest of the night, wallowing in the muddy hay and my guilt. I don't know how long I was in there, but as soon as the sun rose, I heard the truck.

I wasn't the only one who rushed outside. Grandpa Joe and the girls came barrelling out of the house. "Daddy!" Eve yelled as she ran into Eli's arms.

"Hey girls... everything's fine." Exhaustion showed in Eli's voice. "Your mom is still at the hospital."

I stayed far away. They wouldn't want to talk to me. They wouldn't want to look at me. I pulled my inadequate sweatshirt tighter around my neck to block the cold as I watched the events unfold.

"Esther, Eve? Can you girls go into the house please?"

They whined. "Where's Caleb?"

"He's fine," Eli assured. My muscles relaxed.

They went in the house reluctantly. Grandpa Joe moved closer to his son. My ears strained to hear as I stayed hidden by the barn door.

"He's alive, but barely. They said an incredible amount of drugs got into his system." Eli rubbed his face with his hands. Grandpa Joe asked a question, but I didn't hear what it was. Eli's answer told me what it was. "Caleb found—," he paused, choosing his words carefully, "—something that was laced with Xanax."

I couldn't take it anymore. I moved from my frozen state toward the people who were hurting. The ones who had risked it all for me. "It was mine," my timid voice admitted. "I put the drugs in the bottle."

They turned to look at me, pity and anger on their faces. They already knew it was me. Of course they knew. Who else could it have been? I was about to plead for forgiveness when I heard a car door slam louder than ever.

"We know it was you!" Israel's angry voice roared as he trudged through the snow toward me. I was hoping that Eli would step in front of him to protect me, but he stepped aside, allowing Israel to continue on his rampage.

"*How* could you be so selfish? *Foolish?*" His eyes bulging, nostrils flaring, face turning red. I forgot about being cold. I forgot about feeling guilty. I forgot about breathing. Incomprehensible fear took over my nonexistent soul, my racing mind, and even my mutated heart.

"Did you do it on purpose? Since you hate us so much! Does the world revolve around *you?*"

He was a few feet away from me. I crumpled. "I'm—"

I was going to say "sorry," but I was cut off. Israel punched me in the mouth. I barely had time to feel the pain before he yanked me to my feet and threw me against the side of the barn.

"You're *what?* Sorry? Since when is *Robin* sorry for anything? Everyone is out to get him, right? *He's* the victim! Why would *he* be sorry for *anything?*"

I choked on the cold air I was desperately trying to breathe in. My hands were numb, dug into the snow, and a strange pain was developing in the back of my throat. Grabbing the back of my soaked sweatshirt, Israel yanked me up and screamed in my face.

"He could've died! He's a little kid, and he just had his first overdose! You almost killed him!"

The pain in the back of my throat worsened. "I'm sorry!" I croaked, hanging from Israel's strong, menacing arm.

"You're sorry? You think that that fixes it? You were going to kill yourself to fix it, and even that didn't work! *So you think sorry is going to cut it?*"

Another burst of pain came as he slapped me hard with the back of his hand.

"You selfish..."

He hit me again. I saw blood spatter from my mouth onto the spotless white snow.

"Stupid..."

And again. I heard a strange noise.

"*How could you?*" He screamed, punching me in the nose. I heard a crunch before the throbbing pain stabbed at my face once again.

"Israel!" A low, gravelly voice yelled.

He dropped me, and I fell into the blood-stained snow, finally able to discern the strange noise I had been hearing. It was coming from me. Painful, remorseful sobs burst from my chest, causing the unexplained ache in the back of my throat. After years of silence from my emotions, they were all falling apart at once. I couldn't feel anything in my body. My fingers were purple, arms red, sweatshirt soaked with melted snow. Face covered in blood and tears. I was at my lowest, vulnerable, on my knees, weak, in front of the very people who wanted my head on a stake. Or so I thought. Someone dropped to their knees in the snow next to my quivering frame. I looked up. Israel had tears of his own running down his cheeks. Grandpa Joe was standing beside him.

"Robin," Israel's voice was wavering and filled with regret. He put his hands on my burdened shoulders.

"I'm sorry!" I screamed. "I'm sorry for what I did! It was supposed to be me! I didn't mean for him to—," I choked on my words. "Please—forgive me!" I sobbed.

He wrapped his arms around my shaking body and pulled me into his chest. I smelled Grandpa Joe's familiar aftershave and realized he was kneeling beside us, his hand on my head. We sat, freezing cold in the snow, crying. I cried as if I had never cried before.

SICKNESS

I don't remember what happened out there in the snow after that. I guess they must've carried me inside. The very thought of what they must've helped me with makes me sick, because eventually I ended up in dry clothes, clean as a whistle. All I know is I was completely out of it. Hyperventilating and delirious, I tossed and turned in bed, angry, scared, confused, in pain from the beating I had received from Israel, and of course the emotional torture I inflicted upon myself.

I caught a severe chest cold from being soaked in the wet snow. I spent hours coughing up junk, squeezing my eyes shut to try to minimize the migraines, using up whole boxes of tissues and rubbing my nose raw. In between all of that, I had painful bruises and cuts on my face, and I was subjected to bouts of emotional outbursts. Now that I had cried, it was hard to stop. But the tears would only stuff my nose up more, burn my eyes harder, and make my chest ache worse than ever.

When I woke up from my restless sleep, wasted and bleary-eyed, Israel was sitting on the end of my bed, book in hand. I think he had been there the whole time. How long had it been?

"Hey there," he said, closing the book but marking the page with his finger stuck inside. "How do you feel? Can I get you something?"

I didn't know how to look at him or even talk to him. I tried leaning up on my elbows, but I was too weak and I fell back down.

"Hey...just lie there. What do you need?" His gentle hand rested on my clammy forehead. I pushed it away.

"How long have I been sleeping?" I forced myself to ask.

"Three days. But you haven't really been sleeping that whole time. Just the past"—he looked at his watch—"seven hours or so."

I moaned. Being fully awake for the first time gave me a chance to feel how my body was actually doing. I stared at the ceiling and tried to figure out a way to not swallow and save myself the pain. I ended up coughing up a lung.

"Hey...here." Israel handed me a tissue. "I'm going to go get you some lemon and honey." He stood and stretched before heading down the ladder. I heard his bones pop.

I put my hands up to my face, expecting a huge mess from my eyeliner, but nothing came off on my fingers. I rubbed at my eyes again. Same result. No black smudges. I clumsily got out of bed, shivering at my bare feet on the cold floor, and hobbled as best I could over to the mirror. I stared at a stranger. My black hair hung loosely around my face, blond roots obnoxiously showing. My eyes, bright and blue, stood out, as they were not surrounded by a mass of black ink. I saw *her* in my pale, discoloured features. I wanted to smash the mirror. Why had they done this to me? This is what I was trying to hide. My hand instinctively flew up to my head and started messing my hair around, pulling it down in front of my eyes. A dull ache pounded as I pulled harshly on my hair, reminding me I had bruises all over my face and neck. I touched my spilt lip and flinched, remembering what it felt like to be thrown against a wall and smashed in the face by an angry big brother. The barn door opened, and I hobbled back to my bed. I didn't want to have to explain anything.

Israel lumbered up the steps carrying a huge, steaming mug of hot stuff for me. He was taking care of me because I was sick. Again, I remembered her.

"Here ... this will help your sore throat," he said, handing the mug to me with a sympathetic smile. I took it without saying thanks. It didn't bother him. He just sat back against the wall and opened his book.

"Long, long ago, there lived a boy named Kevin, who was his father's favourite son."

I looked up from my scalding hot medicine. "What? You're reading me a fairy tale?"

Israel's eyes never left the page. "No. I'm telling you a story. Do you want to hear it, or do you want to sit there all day, doing nothing but fuss about how sick you feel?"

I felt slightly put down. "Um ... fine. I guess I'll hear it."

Israel nodded and continued with his story. At first, I thought he was reading from his book, but then I realized that he was pulling it out of thin air. "Kevin loved his father. They were the best of friends, always going fishing on the weekends and going out to eat in their favourite diner on the corner of the street. One day, Kevin decided that he was tired of depending on his dad, so he asked him for his share of the will. His father disapproved but gave him the money anyway. Kevin left to make his new life in the big city."

"Are you making this up?" I interrupted. "Or did you get this from a movie? Cause it seems kinda ... Hollywood-ish." I took another sip of the bitter liquid, wishing I didn't sound so cynically ungrateful.

Israel stopped talking and sighed. "No I'm not making it up. But I guess I'll tell it to you some other time since you don't seem to be interested. I'm going to go see if Mom needs help with dinner." With a final confusing glance at me, he left me alone. I felt guilty for insulting his story. I wallowed for a while in self-hatred and pity and eventually forced my deteriorated self to get up and return to the disappointing mirror. I grabbed my black eyeliner pen and smudged it on my eyes. It was like an addiction. If I didn't have it on, if it wasn't hiding me, I felt naked and incomplete. I stared at my face, trying to erase hers from popping up in front of it. I hated it. Sometimes I wanted to gouge out my eyes so I couldn't see her inside of me. My nightmares attacked me from every side. The day I found out she was dying. Her skinny, weak frame lying helplessly in bed. The day she died. The day I found him, self-mutilated and dead. The only thing that I didn't have a nightmare about was the memory of her funeral. But just because I didn't dream about it, didn't stop it from haunting me while I was awake ...

Standing in my black suit, soaked from head to toe, drenched in the rain, I watched her coffin being lowered into the slimy black ground. Marcus was there, but he wasn't holding me. He was lost in his own anguish, comforted by his superficial friends (the same ones who pretended to cry at his own funeral). I was alone. No one knew what to say to me. My mother had just died, and no one knew how to comfort the lost, emotionally dead kid. I didn't cry. I couldn't cry. I had cried so much for her when I found out she had cancer, but crying had never changed the fact she was dying, so I stopped. I squished the mud beneath my feet with my toe, wishing I could suffocate myself with it. I looked around at the people. There were so many of them I didn't know. They didn't care about me, and I didn't care about them. I took off running, I don't know why. Something came over me and I just ran. I heard my name, but I don't know who was calling it. It wasn't my dad. He never noticed anything I did. The rain pelted against my face as I raced to the busy road. I don't remember what I was thinking except for the fact that maybe, just maybe, if I died, I'd see her again. Someone screamed as I skidded to a halt in the middle of the road that was overrun with racing cars, hydroplaning out of control to avoid me. I closed my eyes and waited for the impact, willing the impact. Someone grabbed me and carried me off the road.
"What are you doing?" Justin yelled, slapping my face. I blinked. He had hit me. He had saved me. I didn't want to be saved. I wanted to die ...

I shoved my fists into my eyes and tried to blot out the memory. If only he had just let me die there, none of this would have happened. I wouldn't have suffered. I wouldn't have been hated by my own father and seen him lying in his own blood. I wouldn't have almost killed a little boy and ruined this family's lives. Maybe it would've been better if I hadn't even been born.

I whipped around at the sound of the ladder squeaking, to come face to face with Grandpa Joe and his chessboard. I obeyed as he motioned for me to return to my bed. I sat down. He sat across from me with a grunt and started setting up the pieces. I sighed and tried to force myself to actually care about the game. He obviously loved it, and I had been a jerk when we played. Besides, the mysterious old man sitting in front of me was the only one who stepped in on my behalf the other day in the snow when Israel was pounding me into the ground. The least I could do was play his dumb game with him.

The first three moves were boring and pointless, as we both moved pawns each time. But he then moved his knight into an empty space directly across from my pawn, and I took it without hesitation. He stopped, stunned that I had actually been paying attention. He was expecting me to overlook his unprotected piece like I always did, because I never cared, but this time, somehow, I didn't want to get trampled on. A small smile showed on his wrinkled face as he re-worked his strategy to play against a slightly more formidable opponent. Well, as formidable as anyone can be if the only thing they can do is take one piece before the other player wipes them out. The whole game lasted about forty-five minutes because I wasn't just moving pieces about aimlessly. He still won, but he had to think harder. It felt good. Grandpa Joe chuckled under his breath, gathered up the pieces, and trudged down the ladder and out of the barn.

I wished I could laugh with him and share his tidbit of amusement, but I still didn't understand him or the reason why he always wanted to play the game. I think I decided on the idea I had before: that he just liked to see others lose. My body was starting to shut down again, so I laboriously kicked my way under the covers and lay down. My eyes ached as I dozed for I don't know how long, but it was one of those too-tired-to-sleep moments, and I hated it. My senses perked up as a delicious smell wafted into the room.

"Hey, you ... wake up so you can eat this." Israel set a glass of water down on the nightstand and held a cup of steaming hot something as he sat next to me. My stomach forced me to sit up and see what it was.

"Whuzzinit?" I mumbled, blinking back the tiny knives that were stabbing at my brain and out of my eyes.

"It's beef stew with veggies. Grandma's recipe." Israel held it out to me as I sat up, definitely being lured to it by the mere smell. I took it with weak hands and shoved a spoonful into my mouth. I could barely form words in my mind for how incredible it was.

But I didn't have to. Israel knew I loved it. He had brought a cup for himself, and after his first bite, he mirrored my expression. "So ... I'm going to tell you more of that story."

I didn't care. All I cared about was the succulent food that was gently sliding down my raw and scraped throat. "Sure," I mumbled again, mouth full, my mind wandering in and out as Israel told me what happened to Kevin and the fortune his father had given him.

"He rented the most expensive apartment, bought the most expensive toys and furniture. He drank and partied to his heart's delight, and then one day, he gambled all of it away. Gone. He bet all his money and lost it all. The end."

I was so shocked that Israel had just said, "The end," that I took a deep sharp breath. Not a good idea.

JESUS . . . WHO?

So imagine the most uncomfortable, un-fun, uncontrolled moment in your life. I guarantee it was nothing like mine. I coughed so hard that most of what I was eating ended up on the blanket in front of me. I dropped the cup, spilling its scalding contents all over my legs. After my few minutes of hacking away, my chest felt as if a burning log had fallen on it and caved it in. Israel held me the entire time. He somehow cleaned up the whole mess with one hand. To this day, I have no clue how he did that.

I gave up on understanding his upsetting little story after that. I felt so sick and weak that I just melted into the bed, weary and completely spent. Flat on my back for hours, I fought to keep my lungs from exploding. My blanket and sheets ended up in sweaty clumps after clenching them in my fists. Finally, after an eternity of gasps and wheezes, I drifted into a restless sleep. I dreamed, but it wasn't like anything I had dreamed before.

Everything was black. I was walking down a dark path; something was grabbing at my ankles and feet, trying to trip me up. I ran, but I never moved. The thing that was holding me felt like thorny fingers digging into my skin. I yelled as a sharp pain shot up my legs as I desperately tried to get away. Falling to the unusually soft, damp ground, I tried to crawl away. Icy hands were on me, pulling me in the other direction. Screaming, I kicked at them and tried to pry the fingers off, but their grip just got tighter. A whisper tickled my ear.

"You think I'm gone?" The devilish voice said. "I'm not gone. I'll never be gone. Don't even think about forgetting me. I own you. Just wait."

At first, I thought it was my suicidal heart, but then I realized it was something much more than just me. I was petrified with fear. I couldn't move, couldn't fight as they dragged me farther and farther from where I wanted to go. The only thing I could do was scream.

"Robin …" Israel's voice penetrated my dark dream world.

I yelled for him to help me; I yelled for him to get the prickly hands off my legs and arms.

"Robin, it's a dream! Robin, wake up!"

If it's a dream, why can't I get away? Why aren't I waking up? Why does it hurt so much?

I struggled against the restraining hands, only making it worse. I thought I could see Israel leaning over me, but I couldn't focus on him. I couldn't actually see him. I couldn't wake up.

"Jesus … help him," Israel whispered.

Everything disappeared. The hands let go, the pain faded away, and my eyes opened. Israel was leaning over me, eyes strained, out of breath. "What—," I started to say through a scratchy throat, but Israel stopped me.

"Nightmare. You were having a very real nightmare."

I breathed in as much air as I could. I was free. "Man, that really sucked." I felt my ankle with my toe just to make sure it wasn't shredded. "I couldn't wake up. How did you wake me up?" My eyes adjusted to the dark, and I could see a faint outline of his features.

"Something really had a hold on you. I asked Jesus to help you."

I knew what it was that had had a hold on me. It was the same kind of thing that made me run into the street on the day of my mother's funeral. The same thing that made me destroy Bret's car. Something frightening that I didn't understand. Something that could control me. I tried to shake the panicky feeling that was creeping up my skin again. "Jesus? Caleb's Jesus?"

Israel patted my shoulder with a small, strained laugh. "Yes. Caleb's Jesus. My Jesus. He could be yours too."

"Nah," I said, coughing and turning, with difficulty, to my side. "That's just weird."

"Why?"

"Because that's like saying … well… Ghandi is my Ghandi. I dunno."

Israel got up from my bed and returned to his. "Ghandi? Why him?"

My eyelids were heavy. I wanted to sleep and forget what was controlling me, not discuss this family's weird religion. "Because! Ghandi was a religious smart guy. A teacher, right? Just like this Jesus. Yeah. Big deal. Or Einstein. Or"—I coughed a few times into my pillow—"Darwin or something."

"No." Israel's voice was stern but still gentle. "That's not what Jesus is at all. Jesus is your friend. Your father. Your saviour. He's the son of God, your creator. He watches over you. He loves you."

My mind went crazy. What was all this? I had never heard it before. Jesus? Son of God? That unattainable, unreachable "idea" up in the sky known as God? That just didn't sound real. I tried to sort out logically what Israel had said. If there really was something good and great in this … Jesus … I wanted it.

He said Jesus was my friend. I don't have friends, so that rules that part out. He said Jesus was also my father. Yeah, well, I know what fathers do. They hate you and they leave you. Definitely not interested in that again. What else?

My mind started to blank out as it desperately wanted to sleep, but I wanted to figure this out.

Son of God. Okay, whatever. Um… creator? Why not? Takes less faith to believe in a designer than it does to believe we all just supposedly evolved from a freaking speck.

I knew there was something I was forgetting. Something that I had known to be a lie ...

Loves me! That's it! He said Jesus was my saviour and that he loves me! Well, he did not save me, and he's not saving me now. He doesn't love me. He can't love me. Nobody loves me.

I had figured it out. Jesus was a fake. He was a saviour that let my mother die. He was a father that hated me and abandoned me. He was a friend who stood by and watched as I tried to kill myself. Israel could say all he wanted, but I would know the truth. Jesus, son of God, who loves us all, was just too good to be true. I might have been drowning in my own guilt and despair, but at least I wasn't being deceived.

MOMENT OF CHANGE

My ears perked up. Someone was climbing the ladder. My heavy eyelids opened to see who was intruding on my restless sleep again. Israel had come in a few times that day already to check on me, but I always pretended to be asleep. I didn't want him to bring up his friend Jesus again. I had already lost too much sleep over that matter.

It was Grandpa Joe, and he didn't even wait for me to sit up. He sat on the end of my bed and started setting up his pawns. "Again?" I groaned, immediately coughing up my other lung. In accordance with his usual behaviour, he said nothing. We started playing, as usual, and even though I tried this time to not get pummelled, it didn't work. My mind was somewhere else. I was wondering how many days it had been since they had taken Caleb away. I was wondering if he was okay. I was wondering why Eli or Martha hadn't been up here to check on me. Not that I cared, but it was just weird that *they* didn't seem to care. For once.

"Aww..." my wheezy voice exclaimed as I lost my queen to Grandpa's superior strategy. "I don't know why you play with me. I'm no challenge for you."

He smiled under his grey stubble that was much like his son's and proceeded to checkmate me, watching me, bemused, for my reaction. At first I was annoyed, as usual, but then another sentiment started to sink slowly into my mind. He literally glowed when he played, and he glowed even more at the moment of victory. He was old, probably hundreds of times slower than he was in his early years. What accomplishments did he even have now? Any? Something so simple—like a game of chess—filled him with pride and happiness. Who was I to take that from him, especially since he was taking his time and his energy to spend with me, an unresponsive, disrespectful "whippersnapper."

"Well," I tried to sound cheery, "you did it again. You are just too good for me."

His grin stretched ear to ear as his shoulders shook in silent laughter.

"Hey, Grandpa, Mom has lunch ready," Israel said as he entered the room carrying a tray.

Grandpa Joe gathered up his game and left, one last smile thrown my direction.

"You made him smile. He doesn't smile much," Israel said, unzipping his oversized jacket and kicking off his boots. "It is so cold outside. You're lucky you don't have to go back and forth between the house."

I swallowed as I looked at the heaping pile of food on the tray Israel had brought. I hadn't noticed my stomach growling. Israel grinned at me, the same grin as Grandpa Joe, and sat down on my bed holding the enticing tray.

"I brought us lunch. Are you hungry?"

I nodded, somewhat unable to speak because of my sore throat, and reached for the plate he handed me. Mashed potatoes, beef and gravy, corn, and a warm, buttered bun stared up at me, longing for me to scarf them down. As I ate, Israel talked to me with his mouth full.

"I'm gonna tell you the rest of that story, okay?"

"I thought you said 'the end.' I thought it was over."

"Well, it could've been the end. But it wasn't."

My head was even more confused. "Okay...whatever. So what happened?"

"Let me finish." Israel took a huge forkful of potatoes and

shoved it into his mouth, savouring every chew. "So..." he swallowed. "He had lost everything. All he had were the clothes on his back. He found a job somewhere shovelling garbage into piles. He would pick through it for food when it got dark."

I waved my fork in the air. "This is ridiculous! Everything is going wrong for him! Kicked out? No money? Eating garbage? What kind of story is this?"

"Man, you are so difficult. Just forget it." Israel took a swig of his water and set his empty plate back on the tray.

"Good," I snapped, feeling sorry about it right after. I set my plate on top of his and waited for the awkward silence to pass.

"Here," Israel said, reaching into his bag that was on the floor. "I got you something." He threw a box at me. It was hair dye.

I stared at him. I stared at it. "Why?" I asked, completely astounded that anyone could possibly know how much I had wanted something.

"Because I figured you wanted it. You don't want the blond to show. You're always tugging on your hair as if you hate it. I just thought this might make it better."

"Why—," a violent cough interrupted my words. I struggled to get control of my breathing. "Why," I tried again, "are you doing this?" I coughed again, my chest paining as I heaved, my hands crunching the box.

He handed me a tissue, leaned back on the wall, and brought one of his legs up under him. "Why do you think I'm doing this?"

I blew my nose. I didn't actually need a tissue at that moment. I was just stalling. Why was he turning this already awkward situation on me? I was sick of the lies. Sick of the insinuations. Sick of the assumptions. Sick of the bribes.

"You feel guilty for hating me," I said in a stuffed up voice, looking him in the eyes. No more games.

His eyes glistened and his jaw twitched. He looked away from me and whispered, "Yes."

"Well, don't!" I spat, coughing, dropping the box on the floor and turning on my side toward the wall. I didn't need his pity or his obligatory empathy. I had enough of that from Alice and her government goons back in Miami.

"When my dad told me you were coming, I didn't know what things would be like. I don't like change, and I wasn't looking forward to sharing my room, my life, with a perfect stranger. And when you got here, and I saw you, I panicked. Your eyes were filled with so much hate when you stepped out of the car—I automatically characterized you as a threat."

I didn't want to look at him. I knew he was right. I had been a threat. I still was. He was protecting his family. But then again, I was right too. He had every reason to hate me.

"As I watched you and interacted with you those first few days you were here, I started to realize that you weren't a threat to us, but to yourself."

"That's bull!" I yelled, sitting up as fast as my aching body would allow. "I just about killed your brother!"

Painful compassion filled Israel's eyes as he was about to answer, but a small voice peeped from the bottom of the ladder.

"Israel? Can I come up?"

Israel told Caleb to come, and I sunk into the corner of my bed and pulled the covers close. I had never felt more ashamed than I did right then. Caleb had never hurt me, hated me, or done anything to deserve my wrath, and I had scorned him. Pushed him away. Treated him like garbage. Almost took his young, unfulfilled life. I wished I would pass out from fear before he made it all the way up and I had to face him. It didn't happen.

"Hey, Robin, how are you?" His pale little frame came to the edge of my bed and stared at me, curious, anxious.

I couldn't believe my ears. He looked like death; dark circles around his eyes, a yellowish tint to his skin, and lines that should never be on a child's face marred his kind features. And despite his weakness, he asked how I was. I couldn't answer him. I think I nodded my head.

His angelic smile broke through, completely shattering all remnants of sickness. "Good. I just came up here because I wanted to tell you something."

I waited, barely able to breathe for fear of missing a word.

"I'm so glad it was me because if it had been you, we probably wouldn't have found you in time." He put his little hand on my arm and squeezed. "I thank God it was me."

Israel wiped his own eyes and said something to Caleb, but I don't know what it was. I wasn't listening. I couldn't hear, for my heart was beating too loudly.

Caleb left and I sat there, my arms hugging my knees close to my chest, Israel watching me. Confused tears ached to fall. I tried to fight them, but I wasn't strong enough. Cascading down my cheeks and soaking my blanket, the tears flowed freely, paining my throat.

Israel moved closer to me and reached out his hand. "What is it, Robin?"

Only a strained whisper came out of my mouth. "He thanks God it was him." I didn't understand why, but I didn't have to ask why; Israel already knew I was lost.

"I think he means, he would willingly die if it meant saving your life," he said, putting a hand on my shoulder.

"That's ridiculous!" I shouted, jerking away from him.

"Why?" He grabbed my arms and pulled me back to face him. "Robin, why is it so hard for you to understand that we care?"

"It's not!" I croaked, vainly attempting to pull away from him. He held on and looked at me for the longest time as I cried silently. Slowly, he started to understand.

"Robin, why do you want us to hate you?"

My body started to tremble. Caleb had asked me the same question before, and I had shrugged it off. This time, it affected my entire heart, soul, and mind. My mind wanted to explain, my soul wanted to run away and hide, but my poisoned heart overpowered them all and exploded with rage. Fighting against him, I yelled, "Because you should! My dad hated me! I hate me! There's no reason why you shouldn't..." My chest heaved with pain as I gasped for air.

Israel let me go. "Why don't you want us to love you?"

I turned my tear-soaked face away. "Because I'll love you back."

"What's wrong wi—,"

"People I love *leave me!*" I screamed through my tears. Sobbing, I covered my face in my hands.

Israel grabbed the back of my neck with his hand. His voice wavered as he whispered words I never thought I would hear. "Brother … *I* love you, and I'll never leave you."

My heart broke in two as I sat writhing in pain, sobbing in my brother's loving arms.

NOT EVERYONE FORGIVES

For a moment, I was free. Free of my despair, free of my self-inflicted guilt. Free of my self-loathing and my homicidal heart. For a moment, I had overcome whatever had been driving me, compelling me, to destroy myself. For a moment, I had thought maybe I could carry on. Maybe there was a chance for life to get better. Maybe someone could love me. The moment lasted one day.

It had been a week since Caleb had been rushed to the hospital, and Israel had finally decided that I had hidden in my bed for long enough. He shoved me toward the house while I shied my face away from the pelting snow. "Come on. Get in there. Today is going to be a normal day." I tripped up the steps and fell through the screen door. It was seven in the morning and barely light outside. Israel said he'd drive me to school if I got up and had breakfast with the family. I knew he'd force me to go to school anyway, so I figured if I didn't have to walk I could force myself to sit through a family breakfast. I peeled off my coat and made my way into the kitchen. The gang was all there. My nerves attacked me as usual, but worse this time because the only person who would look at me was Caleb. Ironic isn't it?

"Morning, Robin. Going back to school today?" his little voice said, slightly lower than usual.

"Uh, yeah," I replied, still not able to return his gaze. I sat in my seat and stared at my empty plate.

"How many pancakes would you like, Robin?" Martha asked, emotionless, standing over me with a hot skillet. I knew she wanted to smash me in the face with it.

"One," my little frightened voice squeaked, catching Eli's eye. He smiled politely, and then returned to his newspaper. He was angry with me, and he wanted me out of his house. I looked over at Israel to see if my assessments were right. His avoidance of my gaze assured me that they were. Eve and Esther couldn't stop whispering to each other. I caught a few words here and there. "Can't believe ... still here ... what if ... scary."

Yes, I can't believe it either that I'm still here. No, I'm not going to poison something and give it to any of you. Yes, I know I'm scary.

I ate my pancake in silence and tried not to offend or scare anyone. I couldn't wait to get out of that room, away from the people who still hated me. Caleb may have forgiven me, Israel too, but no one else had. Especially not Martha. Definitely not Martha. My opinion of that was set in stone as I stood up to leave and follow Israel out to the truck.

"Robin, in this house we say please and thank you. It's a common courtesy that is unquestionably required, and you will do so while living in this house," her stern voice scolded.

I felt all eyes on me. "Um ... thank you for breakfast."

"Thank you for breakfast, *what?*" she almost shrieked. I jumped.

"Martha," Eli said.

"Eli, this boy has got to show some respect." Her flaring eyes turned back to me. "Well?"

I wanted to sink into the floor and disappear. "Thank you ... for the breakfast, ma'am?" I guessed at what she wanted to hear.

She nodded her head and poked her girls. "Get up and do the dishes."

I turned and rushed out the door as fast as I possibly could, buttoning my coat on the way to the truck. I jumped in and threw my bag in the back. Nothing could convince me to stay in that house any longer. I wanted to go to school. At school, Martha's condemning and spiteful eyes would not be on me.

The drive was long, bumpy, and freaky as we slid around on the ice, even though there were chains on the tires. I tried to think of one possible way my life would not continue to suck. I couldn't. I was back at the beginning.

"I'm sorry she said that to you, Robin. She was just so scared when—," Israel tried to console.

"She hates me," I said, leaning my face against the cold glass window.

He didn't answer, and I knew it was because he thought there was a really good chance that his mother really did hate me at the moment. "What time do you want me to come get you?" he said, pulling up to the school. At least, I think it was the school. I could barely see through the thick snowfall.

"As soon as possible." I slammed the door without waiting for an answer and ran inside. Unfortunately, I had forgotten that Two Hills was a tiny town, and the fact that everyone knew everything about everybody escaped my mind. But as soon as I walked in that classroom, the precious fact jumped up and bit me in the face. The girls who were glued to their cell phones took one look at me, and their phones started clicking more furiously than ever—probably spreading the news to everyone in the school that I was back. The jocks took a break from staring at them, glared at me, and then continued to ogle. The fat kid sat with his mouth open in shock and horror, food half chewed on his tongue. The kid in the baseball cap actually woke up and watched me as I made my way to my seat in the back; the furious typing of the computer nerd telling me he was writing an essay on my behaviour. Alex and Max were not there, but River was. He gave me one look, telling me that if I squealed on them about the drugs I would die, and then looked back down to his PS3. I sat and locked gazes with Mr. Penner. I wanted to laugh at his obvious dilemma. Should he smile at me? Say something? Ignore me? What a loser.

He eventually started his tedious lecture, and I found a happy place. I had not planned to be in that class again, and I was quickly remembering why I had felt a strange sense of glee at that morbid thought. The bell rang, and I waited for the class to file out before I left. I didn't want to walk in front of them all again.

"Robin, it's been a while. How are you?" Mr. Penner asked.

I stopped at his desk and flung my red bag over my shoulder. "I'm here, aren't I?"

He was caught off guard. His little beady eyes widened in fear of his lack of words. "Um ... I ... well, one thing," he started shuffling papers on his desk. "About your exam ... I was wondering if you would like to take it again."

I scoffed. "No."

"Well," He pushed his coke-bottle glasses up on his shiny nose. "You did repeat the ninth grade. Do you want to be stuck in the tenth grade forever?"

My anger flared. He was blowing on my dying embers. "No," I seethed.

"Well then ... let's find a good time this week to retake it." He smiled at his triumph. Why did everyone find pleasure at my annoyance?

"Whatever." I left him fiddling with his schedule and started to head toward my next class. I had barely made it five steps before I heard my name.

"Oh, Robin," the three Barbie dolls surrounded me. "Um ... listen ... about the Christmas Banquet ... we think we're going to go with someone else."

"Thank God," I said sarcastically, pushing past them and their perfect selves. "I couldn't imagine a worse torture."

I don't think they heard me, for they followed me. "So ... did you ... really like ... try to kill that little boy?"

I spun around. "What do you think?" I spat.

They squealed and hurried away. "See? I told you ..." they whispered to each other.

I had enough. "What did you say?" I yelled after them. They turned around, horrified, along with everyone else in the hallway.

"You think I tried to kill him? Why? 'Cause I'm an American? Cause I wear black clothes?"

Their faces went stark white as they shook their heads, trying to appease the monster that had broken loose. I swore at them as loud as I could.

"Picking on girls now, eh, *Emo Boy?*" A sickly voice said. My body was slammed up against the lockers as the two seniors who I had pummelled stared down at me.

I swore at them too. Big mistake.

One of them bashed his hand into the locker right next to my head. The other one grabbed my jaw. I struggled against his power, but he was even stronger than Israel. "Not so feisty now, eh? Let's see how a nice long stay in this locker calms you down, and then maybe you can learn how to talk to girls civilly." The metal door screeched as they yanked it open. I fought as they shoved me inside, but I only ended up hurting myself even more. They slammed the door shut, squishing me in the tightest, most uncomfortable space I had ever been in. I couldn't move a muscle. My face ached from where he had gripped me. I tried to push to try to budge the door open, but it was useless. It had been locked. Hence the word *locker.* I wanted to scream at myself for losing my temper, for letting myself be caught off guard by the seniors. But I knew I deserved to be stuck in there after what I had done to them.

They left me in there for one whole class period. I know that, 'cause the bell rang and everything got quiet. Then after ages went by, the bell rang again, and my locker opened. I fell out backwards right into their destructive hands. Dragging me into the bathroom, they laughed and joked with each other about the events of the day so far, not even giving me a second thought. They took turns punching me, alternating my face and my stomach. I don't know how long that lasted. They took me back to my prison and shoved me inside. Blood ran down my face and onto my lips as everything in my body ached. Again. At least I didn't have to struggle to hold myself up. The confining locker walls did that for me.

"Have a nice day, *Emo Boy*," one of them said. "You'll have a long time to think about what you did to those girls and that little kid."

Yes, I was in there all day. I don't know how I survived it. The blood dried thick and crusty on my face, my legs fell asleep, my arms fell asleep. The only thing that did not fall asleep was me, unfortunately. At last, I heard someone fiddling with the lock on my locker of death. The door swung open and I fell out into someone's arms. Israel. I clung to him, as I could barely stand.

"Oh, Robin..." he said, holding me up.

"Can we just go?" I groaned.

He helped me outside into the truck. I fell asleep on the way home.

THE RIGHT CROWD

So it turned out that the fact Israel had come and rescued me only made things worse. The next day when I went to school, I got my head stuck in a toilet—for the first time in my life. What do they call them? Whirlies? Swirlies? I wasn't used to that, being treated like a nerd/outcast. Fortunately, that was Friday, so I got a break from being bullied. But what I couldn't decide was which was worse: swirlies from bullies or a goody-two-shoes youth group. That's what Eli sprung on me on the way to church. A youth group. I heard him telling Martha he wanted to get me involved with some kids who would have a "good influence" on me. I also heard her telling him she didn't think Mother Teresa herself could be a good influence on me.

I sunk lower into my seat in the back of the van, the seatbelt choking the life out of me. Good.

"It's not that bad, Robin," Caleb said. "The people there are really nice once you get to know them."

Poor kid. He was so naïve. All of those churchgoers hated me, and now they would hate me even more because of what I had done. Israel knew that. I could tell. He gave me a sympathetic smile and whispered in my ear. "Some people just don't take the time to see what's beyond their assumptions."

I shrugged. I didn't really care. I didn't want people to "see beyond their assumptions" and look into my soul. Israel and Caleb had, but that was enough. I didn't think I could handle anyone else on the inside.

"Besides, I'll be there at youth group with you. You'll like it. We have pizza." Israel nudged my arm and straightened out his tie. Yeah. He wore a tie. I didn't even own a tie anymore.

We got to the little church and were ushered inside by the people trying to get out of the cold. The familiar musty smell made me scrunch up my nose. I eyed the ridiculously uncomfortable pews with sorrow, as I knew I would soon be sitting in one for a few hours. Patrick Friesen barrelled over to me. I tried to sink into the walls, but Israel stopped me from moving. I hated it when he did that.

"Robin! How are you doing?" His booming voice probed as he towered over me.

I wanted to laugh in his face. How was I doing? Utterly absurd question.

"I heard from Israel that you're coming to our youth group tonight. That's great!" He stuck his fist out to me. What? Did he think he was cool trying to *fist-bump* me? Did he think he was ghetto? Did he think he was lowering himself to my level? No way was I going to allow him to "reach" me.

"Whatever." I shrugged and looked around for Israel. He had left me standing there with Patrick, alone and defenceless. I wanted to get away from him before he started to psychoanalyze me again.

"This way, Robin."

A pure jolt of electricity coursed through my body as Caleb took my icy fingers in his warm hand. I didn't want him touching me. In other words, I didn't feel worthy to touch him. He led me to a pew in the middle of the sanctuary, and I slid in next to Israel, the front of the church, back of the church, and both sides of the church staring at me. I calmed the butterflies in my stomach once Caleb had let go of me and the pastor got everyone's attention.

Yes, I'm back. Everyone stare. No, please do. Oh wait, you can't see

me? Do you want me to stand up and wave? There you go. It's me!
The suicidal maniac! The gothic boy who tried to kill the innocent
child. I'm sorry I'm soiling your perfect holy pews by sitting on them.
Trust me; I'd leave right now if my wardens would let me.

"Let's all take a few moments to welcome each other," the
pastor said. The entire congregation stood up, and I froze. Israel
made me stand up. I stood there, willing the excruciating moment
to be over. I felt a hand on my arm.

"Child … it's a pleasure to have you worship with us today." A
tiny old woman leaned over the pew in front of me and took my
hands. She pulled me into her body and hugged me, her jewellery
poking into my neck, her perfume wafting up my nose. I was so
shocked, I let her do what she wanted.

She pulled back and touched my cheek with her wrinkly,
ring-clad fingers. "You have such pretty eyes. My husband had
those eyes."

My throat closed up. My mother's eyes. She could see them.

"God bless you, child." She smiled a tender smile and sat back
down. Israel had to push me into my seat. My eyes were welling
up with tears. I blinked them away furiously and fiddled with my
own rings on my fingers. I could still feel her gentle hand on my
face. I looked around for the evil looks I had assumed everyone
had for me. No one scowled. No one rolled their eyes. They nodded at me, smiled, winked even. I felt welcome and loved.

When the service was over, I lost count of how many people
came to me and hugged me. I had no idea why. Why the first
time I had felt such hostility and judgement, and how it had all
changed. It felt amazing. But… only for a moment. All good
things only last for a moment, don't they? My heart fell back
to the pit it had been festering in when I saw them, about five
young people, older than me, standing off to the side, glaring
straight at me. Whispering among themselves and pointing at
me, arms crossed. I knew they saw me for what I had done. Israel
tried to get me to forget about them, but I couldn't. They were
right. I had no right to be in their church. I was as big a sinner

as I could possibly be. I don't know why I even bothered to hope that the Christians might not hate me after all.

Israel and I were still arguing about it as evening fell and the time for youth group had come.

"Robin, they're stupid teenagers. They don't—"

"They don't what?" I interrupted. "Judge me? Don't tell me that, 'cause that'd be a lie. I know when people hate. I *know*." I fell silent as we drove the rest of the way to the church. I didn't want to go back there. I wanted to be in the comfort of my safe, warm bed. The only place where no one would stare. The only place I felt the tiniest bit of peace.

Israel didn't say anything else either. He knew his words were falling on deaf ears. He pulled around to the back of the church. The engine died with a shudder. Kind of how my life force felt at that moment. "Let's go," he said, getting out of the truck.

I jumped out into the crunchy snow and slammed the door. I didn't even have to try to show my bitterness at being where I didn't want to be. It came out naturally. The one thing I hoped for was that those whispering, pointing teenagers would not be there.

They weren't. There was one person I recognized, however. In the middle of the room, in the basement of the church, between the pool table and the foosball tables sat the boy with the baseball cap who slept in my biology class. He was on a big brown bean-bag chair, laughing at the top of his lungs at one of his friends who was trying to crush a soda can on his forehead. Israel saw where I was looking.

"That's Peter. He's a genius. You've probably seen him sleeping in class. That's because when he gets his books for his classes, it takes him about half an hour to read each one. And when I say read, I mean memorize." Israel took my coat from me and hung it up with his before ushering me into the middle of the room filled with about twenty teenagers. I wanted to sink into a dark abyss somewhere.

"Hey, guys. You made it," Patrick said, slapping Israel on the back and looking at me. He knew better than to slap me on the back. "Tonight's kinda laid back. We'll play a few games, and then people can just eat and hang out."

If my stomach could twist any harder, or my nerves race any faster, they would have. A group game. That meant no sitting in my own world, ignoring everyone. Israel ushered me into the circle of chairs the kids had set up, and I plopped down in one, determined that whatever they were going to do would suck. Israel did not sit next to me. I almost panicked, but then I tried to force myself to remember that I was not a baby, and I didn't need him to hold my hand. I did do my best to send off signals that I was not into talking to anyone. It didn't work. Peter sat next to me, and on the other side, a girl with long blonde hair and sunglasses on top of her head, even though it was nighttime.

"Hi," she said, extending her hand to me. "I'm Lynnette. I've seen you around, but I don't remember your name."

I took her hand and winced at her strong, un-girl like grip. "Um ... Robin."

"Oh yeah, that's right." She smiled and flicked her fingers through her bangs. "Israel's cousin from Miami. Julio Iglesias once had five gallons of water flown from Miami to L.A. so he could wash his hair."

I had never heard anything so random in my life. There must've been something wrong with her. Lynnette turned to talk to whoever was sitting on her other side when Peter spoke up.

"She's been homeschooled all her life."

I turned to look at his teasing face. "What?"

"She's the epitome of a homeschooler! A useless fact within five seconds of meeting a new person," Peter chuckled. "But she's really awesome. I like her."

I still had a hard time understanding how two people who didn't even know me could talk so easily to me, without annoyance, disgust, or fear. I sat up a little straighter in my chair.

"You're in my bio class, aren't you?" Peter asked me.

"You noticed me?"

He smiled and locked his cap to one side. "Ah, just because I look like I'm sleeping doesn't mean that I am. You know what I mean?"

"More than you can imagine." I sighed, realizing I had just said something extremely revealing.

"All right everyone!" Patrick yelled over the chattering. "We're gonna play charades, but first, we have someone new joining us. Israel, do you want to introduce him?"

Israel broke his conversation away from two girls who were hanging on him and cleared his throat. "This is my second cousin, Robin. Tell them something about you."

Sheesh. He was talking to me.

"Tell us a bit about yourself, Robin," Patrick urged. I guessed I was past the stage where everyone tiptoed around me.

"Uh..." I racked my brain for something I could say that wouldn't scare them. "Hi...I'm Robin..."

"Hi, Robin!" they all chimed together, catching me off guard. I felt like I was at an AA meeting.

"Uh...it's been three weeks since my last confession."

Every single one of them laughed, not at me, but at what I said. It felt so good.

"I'm from Florida. I've never seen snow before in my life."

More laughter. Good laughter.

"That's all," I said, crossing my arms and slinking back down in my chair. Israel beamed at me.

"Great, great. You'll all have a chance to talk to Robin later, but now let's get on with the game!" Patrick numbered the group off in two teams and picked Peter to go first.

The whole thing was a mess. People were screaming, guessing at the wrong times, cheating, and laughing. I didn't guess, I didn't go up there, but I did smile. The homeschooler, Lynnette, was hilarious. She was trying to act out the word *circus*. Yeah. Just imagine.

After it was over, we all got pizza and Coke. It tasted so good. I loved Martha's cooking, but every once in a while one needs some good, solid, unhealthy, junk food. At first, Lynnette tried to start a conversation with me, but we both decided it was useless after five minutes of *nothing in common*. She wanted to talk about "Nocturne in E flat Minor," Larry Norman, and Awana, but since I had no real clue as to what any of those were, we parted, mutually agreeing that the conversation had gone on laboriously long enough. Peter, however, knew what those things were, and he didn't care. What he did care about was music.

"I started playing the guitar when I was about nine. It was frustrating though, because my fingers could barely reach the chords," he said, stuffing the last bit of pizza into his mouth.

I downed the rest of my Coke and nodded in agreement. "Yeah... it was a while before I could play bar chords. I have smaller hands."

His eyes widened. "You play?"

"Yeah."

He threw his plate down, grabbed my sweatshirt, and pulled me to the corner of the room. My heart pounded in excitement at the sight of his guitar. He thrust it into my hands. "Play something!"

I took it and caressed its frame. Sleek and perfect. How long had it been since I'd played music? I pulled a chair closer to me with my foot and sat down. My fingers automatically flew over the strings. I didn't care who was watching or listening. I was finally holding an instrument again. I played. What? I don't know.

Lynnette rushed excitedly over and sat cross-legged in front of me. "You play the guitar? I knew we had *something* in common!"

A light went on in my head. *Nocturne in E flat Minor.* "Oh..." I said. "You play the piano." I chuckled a bit at my stupidity.

"Yeah! But I can't play the guitar. I can't play by ear, so... I wouldn't know any of the contemporary stuff that you know."

A guy with a massive head of curly blond hair picked up the bass guitar that was leaning on the wall. "Play something, dude. I'll join in."

I didn't even have to think about what to play. I decided to play something for her. As I plucked out *Greensleeves,* she squealed and closed her eyes, slowly swaying back and forth. The bass guitar followed me better than ever. I was in heaven. It felt even better when the whole room applauded when I finished. They had all been listening.

Peter put his hand on my shoulder. "Man, you play classical? That's pretty sweet. What else do you play?"

Suddenly, my eye caught something I hadn't seen before. Peter followed my gaze. "You play drums?"

"Yeah," I whispered, handing his guitar back to him. "But it's been a while."

"Well, come on then!" He said, flinging his guitar around his shoulder. "Let's play some!"

Lynnette shoved me forward as the bass guitar whined. I approached the drum set apprehensively as someone thrust a pair of sticks into my hands. Could I still play? Did I still want to play? The last time I had been behind a set, I had totally destroyed it. As soon as I sat down, all the doubt disappeared. I looked at Israel one last time before hammering out a rhythm that the crowd loved. He had his hands in the air, his eyes closed, and his lips were moving. I guessed he was praying to his God. Alan, the bass guitar player's name that I learned later, Peter, and I played music well into the night. I never wanted to leave.

ABOUT FACE

Monday morning had never looked so good. I had no nightmares plaguing my sleep after youth group. For the first time in years, people liked me. They didn't pity me, scorn me, judge me, or avoid me. They spoke to me, genuinely interested in who I was, not what I looked like, did, or what I had most recently gone through. Was it because they didn't know? Or was it because they didn't care?

It was a beautiful, freezing day outside, and I opted to walk to school. Israel raised his eyebrows in surprise and then gave me a sideways hug. I flinched away still. I guess I just wasn't used to someone treating me like they cared about me. It had been too long. "Don't get in trouble today, Robin," he yelled after me as I trudged through the sparkling snow.

My contentment faded. Of course I would get in trouble. There was no way I could avoid Alex and his gang, and the seniors would most definitely think up something horrific to do to me. But then a light appeared in the darkness. Peter would be there! Maybe if I stuck with him, they wouldn't get me.

I arrived a few minutes late for biology and was seriously considering skipping out, but as I peered in the window of the classroom, Mr. Penner saw me and rushed to open the door. "Come in, Robin. I was just taking attendance."

I groaned inwardly and inched my way in the door. Peter smiled at me as I made my way to my chair in front of three pairs of confusing eyes. I smiled back, feeling slightly comforted, but my mind raced with what Alex and the guys were thinking. Peter put his head down on the desk and started to fall asleep, and my mind wandered back to the music we had played the night before. I longed to be holding the drumsticks and beating away all my stress, the music carrying me away to a place where everything was perfect. A place where my mom was.

"Robin," Mr. Penner said, waking me up from my fantasy, "can I see you a moment?"

Class was over. I had daydreamed the whole thing away. I stood and shuffled to his desk. "Yeah, what?"

"Today after school would be a good time to retake the exam. You have to get it done before Christmas break. Midterms are coming up." His beady eyes widened. I could tell he dreaded grading midterms as much as his students dreaded taking them.

I muttered, "Fine," and followed Peter, who had been waiting for me, out of the room.

"Hey, Robin, whassup?" Peter asked, grabbing my hand and shaking it hard. "How are you?"

I couldn't help but smile. "I'm okay. You?"

Peter adjusted his ball cap and stretched out his arms. "I'm tired. And bored. Sometimes I wish I didn't have to come to school."

"Right, cause you know all this stuff already," I said. I hoped I wasn't sarcastic.

"Only by the grace of God." His face shone as he spoke. "He's given me the gift of learning, and I can't wait to use it for his glory."

I rolled my eyes. These people were so far gone.

"What class do you have next?" he asked.

Before I could answer, someone grabbed my sleeve and pulled me over to the lockers. "Hey, bird boy. What's this I heard about you giving my stuff to a little kid? Hey man, that's not cool," Alex seethed in my face.

Peter tried to shove him away, but River pushed him back.

"I didn't give it to him, Alex. He accidentally got some." I stood my ground. No way was he going to bully me like the others did. I could beat the tar out of him, and I would if he started it first.

"Oh did he? Well, you'd better be right, 'cause if anyone found out that stuff came from me … you'd be so dead."

"Get lost, Alex," Peter warned.

"Shut up, Benny Hinn. I'm just talking to my friend Robin here. This ain't none of your business. See you later, bird boy." Alex shoved me into the locker with a slam and left with his cronies down the hall.

"What was he talking about, Robin?" Peter asked, worry lines marring his face.

I straightened out my sweatshirt and started down the hall. "Nothing. I don't know. I gotta go to class."

I didn't hear him say anything as I walked down the hall. He was probably too busy thinking about what it was that had just happened.

Great. I knew those church kids all liked me because they didn't know what I had done! Now Peter knows, and he'll tell them, and they'll treat me like everyone else treats me. Like a freakin' convict.

The rest of the day was hell. Everyone had heard the story of "innocent, overdosed Caleb and the evil boy with emo hair." If they hadn't heard it before, Alex and his gang had surely told them. The only thing that was going for me was that I hadn't seen the seniors at all. Anywhere. As I sat down in the biology room once more to retake the exam, I felt relieved. The day was over. All I had to do was put some bogus answers on the dumb test and I could go home. Or so I thought.

"Here you go, Mr. Cane," Mr. Penner said. I winced. Mr. Cane was my dad, not me. I looked down at the familiar papers stapled together and read the first question.

"Write the names of ten out of the fourteen classification groups in the animal kingdom.

I laughed and wrote the exact same answer I did before.

crustaceans, mammals, bugs, birds, fish, rodents, girls, canadians, mounties, your mom

I looked at the next question, but instead of tossing my pencil away as I had done before, I made up something quick and
scribbled it in the blank space. If it looked as though I "answered"
every question, he'd at least let me leave the room. After about
twenty minutes, I picked up my paper and my bag, plodded over
to his desk, and dropped my test in front of his face.

"There you go," I said cheerily. "Can I go now?"

He sighed and rubbed his forehead. "Well, if you think you
spent enough time on it ... "

I spun on my heels and left the room. No way was I going to
spend more time on his stupid test. Oh, if only I had.

"We've been waiting for you," a low voice sang eerily just
before I was knocked off my feet and dragged into the bathroom.
It was dark. The lights had been turned off in the main hallways
for the night already, but I knew it was the seniors. There were
three of them this time, and there was no chance of escape. I
prepared myself to fight.

They shoved me against the wall and locked the door. The
light flipped on as I turned around to face them. The senior I
had never seen before stared at me with livid eyes. He scared me
more than anything I had ever been scared of before. He looked
like me. His eyes had the same hate as mine had when I looked
in the mirror. I backed up against the cold, dirty tiles on the wall,
unable to speak.

"Hey, Robin," one of them said, "we just thought we'd all have
a little chat. This here is Mitch." The senior pointed to the one
who watched me with hate. "You know what's bugging him?"

I stuck my chin up in the air, trying to force the look of courage. "What?"

"Well, when he was a kid, his pop tried to kill him by slipping him something lethal."

I wanted to scream for help. I knew what would happen next. This guy, this—mirror image of me was going to kill me because of what I had done. I knew it was bound to happen sometime. But what would I do? Would I stand there and let him crush me into the wall? Or should I stand up for myself?

The other senior laughed obnoxiously and grabbed a handful of my hair in his fist. "Hey, guys, did you see that Robin here looks like Mitch?" He yanked my head back so they could see my face.

"That little punk looks nothing like me!" yelled Mitch.

My fire raged inside me. I elbowed the guy holding me in the stomach as hard as I could. He let go with a painful whoosh. The other two laughed while the one I had injured tried to regain his balance.

"Feisty, isn't he?" the first senior said to Mitch.

"For now," Mitch replied and reached out for me. I slapped his hand away, backing up as fast as I could. They would not take me quietly. I never noticed I was backing up right into the senior I had just elbowed. A sharp pain stabbed me in my side, and I sank to my knees. He had punched me with all his might right in the kidney. Mitch fell to his knees in front of me and stuck his demonic face in front of mine. "So I guess we've never met. I'm Mitchell Newman. I believe you know my brother, Bret. He knows you."

As the pain would not subside, I had to rack my brain to think of whom he was talking about. I wanted to cry like a baby when I realized he was talking about Bret: the cop who wanted me dead.

"Yeah," he said, seeing the terrified recognition on my face. "*That* Bret. He's told me all about you, kid. About your constant annoyance, how you badmouth him and call him insulting names. About how you beat up my friends here ... it's just unacceptable."

My mouth ran away with me. "Oh yeah? What are you gonna do about it, you pansy?"

He smiled for a moment, and then all I saw was black. He had hit me in the face with his forehead. I think it hurt too much to actually feel it.

"You know, I read your file, Robin Cane. I know all about you. I know about your mommy and your daddy, and how you tried to rid the world of your pathetic existence. If you ask me, you didn't try hard enough."

I held my head in my hands and tried to avoid his eyes. Every time I looked into them, I saw myself. I saw what I was inside. I saw what I hated most.

"It's no wonder your mommy left you. Look at you. Trembling. Wallowing."

"Shut up!" I screamed through my pain.

"And your daddy? Crap. If you were all I had left in this world, I'd kill myself too."

"All right, Mitch. Let's go," the others urged.

"No. I'm not done with this pinhead." Mitch grabbed my face and made me look at him. "Why are you here? Everyone hates you. Everyone wants you gone. You're worth nothing. So just finish what you started. Do the world a favour and rid it of you, or I'll come back and do it myself."

He pushed me away from himself and stood up, brushing off his pants from the dirty bathroom floor. "Let's go, boys. Robin Cane has learned his lesson. His last one."

The seniors actually looked remorseful as they glanced at me one last time before heading out the door behind Mitch.

I sat, legs numb, head throbbing, blackened heart thriving. Why had I even bothered to think things would change? Why had I believed all the lies? I was the scum of the earth, and the only thing that could be done was to scrape myself off it. I stood, shaking and freezing, and started outside. The icy wind hit me like a wave crashing on a pit of fire. I ran home as fast as I could, snow biting at my already raw skin. Everything Mitch had said was true, and his words rang over and over in my ears as I scrambled up the ladder and collapsed on my bed.

You're worth nothing. Everyone hates you. Finish what you started.

A familiar, bone-chilling voice joined the jumble of words.

I'm still here. Are you ready to let me in? Let me in. Let me in.

The prickly hands scratched at my skin once more, dragging me down. Only this time, Israel wasn't there to save me. I felt it pressing on my chest, choking me, and hurting me. It crushed the air out of my lungs, forcing me to take a sharp breath and breathe it in. It crept in my nostrils and filled the back of my throat. Once it had made its way in my body, I slept. Deeply.

THE BEGINNING OF THE END

"You can't make him go back! Can't you see what they're doing to him?" Israel's voice carried through the crack in the window. I listened, lying still on my bed, to the argument between Eli and Israel.

"Israel, keeping him out of school is not an option."

"But Dad, we can teach him at home."

"You remember his first reaction to that! It would never work!"

"Dad—"

"No!" Eli yelled louder than I had ever heard him yell. What was it in his voice? Fear? I heard footsteps approach the ladder down below and slowly climb. I thought it was Israel. I sat up to face him and saw that it wasn't Israel but Eli. My body seized up.

"Robin ..." he started, rubbing his beard and searching for the right words. "I'm not sure about everything that's been going on with you, but what I do know is ... you have to return to school. Martha and I are spent, Robin. We don't know what else to do with you. If you don't go back, you'll have to leave.

Even though I knew that's what he was going to say, it still stung. Go back to hell on earth, or leave the only place that I knew? The only place that I had?

"Well?" Eli grew impatient.

"I'll go," I whispered, because I knew if I used my voice it would break, and he would see me cry. He left and I sat up. I couldn't think. Nothing formulated in my mind. It was completely blank. I didn't know how things could possibly get any worse. As I debated getting up and throwing myself out of the window, my eyes rested on the little box that was halfway underneath my bed. I picked up the hair dye and went to the sink. It was like watching someone else dye their hair. I was running on autopilot. My arms moved robotically around my head as I squished the dark liquid into my hair, the bitter chemicals stinging my nose and throat. Slowly, the inch of disgusting blond hair disappeared, covered in ink. A surge of satisfaction tingled in my fingers and toes, knowing that I could again hide who I was, what I was. As I washed it out, the water swirled black and thick down the drain. I felt like I was losing my very being down that drain.

I rubbed the towel roughly on my head, wishing I could rub away the pain. Looking up into the mirror, Mitch's face was in the place of my own—evil, threatening, and distorted. I cringed and looked away, the pain in my head becoming all the more severe. I blindly stumbled back to the bed, completely oblivious to the fact that Israel had been standing behind me for a long time.

"So…" he said, sitting on his favourite place at the end of my bed. "Kevin was living on the streets with no money and no one to help him survive."

I started listening. There wasn't anything else I could do.

"So he decided to go back to his father and beg for him to give him a job," Israel continued, his voice getting quieter. "Kevin was convinced that his father would turn him away, but it was his only option. When he got close to home, his father ran out to meet him, overjoyed."

"What?" I asked, breathing heavily into my pillow.

"His father forgave him, brought him back into his home, and threw a party to celebrate his return."

Lies, I thought. *All lies.*

"He was so happy that his son, who was lost, was then found."

"You know what, Israel?" I thrust myself off the bed and yelled in his face. "Just shut up about your special *Kevin* and his redemption story! I don't want to hear about how his life worked out just fine and how mine is shot to hell!"

"Robin—"

"No!" I yanked on my wet hair. "I don't want to hear it! Your constant patronizing and … false hope!" The tears were coming. "I'm tired of everyone telling me it will "work out" or "be okay" when it doesn't and won't!"

"But you haven't given him a chance, Robin!" Israel said, standing up.

"He's—not—real—Israel! Your *Jesus* is not here!" I could feel the familiar, unwelcome force taking over, polluting my mind. I calmed myself by clasping my hands over my mouth and sitting down. Israel sat next to me gently.

"Robin—"

"Don't," I spat. "Just stop. Leave me alone."

He left, and I cried. I had lost all shreds of hope I had gained in the last few days. I was completely at a loss for what to do next.

DEAD ZONE

Christmas. That word meant nothing to me except for that it was a week from Saturday, and that meant I only had three days of school left. Did I skip ahead too far? Are you with me? Let me go back and explain the last few weeks.

I had gone back to school, yes, and it was better and worse. The two seniors who had at first started bullying me actually left me alone. It was Mitch who made it a living hell. It wasn't the same kind of torture as the seniors had inflicted, such as swirlies and being crammed into a locker, but it was a form of torture that was far worse. Every day that he saw me, he'd ask me, "You're still here? I thought you would have offed yourself by now." He knew things about my parents. About my mom's cancer, how sick she looked just before she died. He knew things that my dad had said to me when he was grieving for her and resenting me.

> *"How did it feel when your mommy couldn't even get up the strength to hug you? How did it feel when your daddy said he wished you'd never been born? When he looked right into your eyes and didn't even have to say anything for you to know he hated you? When he didn't say a word to you for months?"*

That's what he would say. How did he know those things? I didn't know, but every time he came near me, the pain and hurt would just ache and cut deeper. I think my mutated heart and my blackened soul were tired of trying to destroy me and started to destroy themselves instead.

Eli had said nothing about going to church as a condition of staying at the farm, so I refused to go. They gave up trying to force me, so they went without me. I didn't go back to the youth group either. I couldn't stand facing them, knowing that they despised me for tricking them and deceiving them, and that they knew the truth about me. I longed to be back with them; playing music, laughing, without my shame … without my … sin.

Eli and Martha barely spoke a single word to me except when I had done something unacceptable. They didn't trust me, and every time they even glanced in my direction, I could feel their hurt by my betrayal of that trust. Caleb would still talk to me all cheery and kind, but I could never muster a response. The guilt was unbearable.

Grandpa Joe had come once to play chess, but I didn't even move the first piece. I annoyed him and worried him. He grunted at me angrily at first for not taking my turn, but then he looked into my eyes and saw what I was feeling. I knew he saw what I was feeling because his eyes misted up as he put away his game, unplayed. He then did something that I will remember in my heart and in my life forever. He put his old hand on my head and closed his eyes, his lips moving fervently as he prayed. My entire body seized up and wanted to implode, a massive mix of confused emotions wanting to run wild. I don't know how long he sat there with me.

Israel hadn't given up on me, even though it seemed as if Eli and Martha had. I had screamed at him and told him to leave me alone, but he didn't. He still brought me food—which I didn't eat—and talked to me, but I never said a word for fear of breaking down in a heap of emotions. Every night he would pray out loud for me as we lay in the dark. At first, I listened because the words sounded so nice, but eventually I plugged my ears. I was tired of broken promises and false hope. He knew I wasn't listening, but he still prayed every night just the same.

Midterm exams. That's what the last three days of school before Christmas break consisted of. Most of my classmates hated them, dreaded them, but I didn't care. I was failing every class with flying colors; what would a midterm grade mean to me?

"Did you study, Robin?" Peter asked. He had been so faithful in saying hello to me and being a friend, but I was so consumed in my own guilt that I completely shut him out.

I shook my head no as I sat in my seat and stared at the massive bundle of papers that were waiting for me.

"Hey, listen..." Instead of sitting in his usual seat in the corner, he sat in front of me and leaned over. "Um...is there a reason why you haven't been to youth group in a while?"

I thought up a lie really quickly. "I've been busy with homework," I said, unwrapping the snow-soaked scarf from around my neck. I shivered as bits of it dripped down my collar.

Peter wanted to tell me that he knew I was lying, but he held his tongue, probably because he didn't want me to shut him out completely. All he said was, "Hmm..."

The two hours we had to take our biology midterm dragged on forever. Out of one hundred questions, I knew the answers to probably twenty-five. Do you know what it's like to have two whole hours to do nothing but sit and think about how much of a loser you are? Do you know how it feels to realize that your life really is nothing more than a pathetic waste of space? The most I would get on that midterm was 25 percent, completely re-affirming the fact that I was a failure.

The bell rang, and I handed in my scribbled-on, mostly blank test, knowing that they would probably kick me out of school.

"So, hey..." Peter called after me as I was heading toward my next midterm. "The reason I was asking about youth group was 'cause the guy in our band who played drums moved. And we need someone to play. Do you want to join us?"

Crisis. My brain knew I would jump at the offer, which

was something I was missing in my life, but absolutely none of my other senses even twitched at the news. I felt no desire, no impulses, no yearning for the thing I had once longed for.

"I can't," I said. Something inside my head screamed at me for making the wrong decision, but it quickly faded away.

Peter was shocked. So was I.

"Um…okay, well…if you change your mind, let me know…'cause we really need someone with talents like yours." He smiled awkwardly and sadly and ran down the hall to his next class.

Why don't I want to play? Why can't I feel anything? Why is everything dead inside?

I fought with myself all day, wondering what it was that was controlling my will. Or maybe nothing was controlling me and I had just changed. But no matter how I tried to justify it, I knew what it was. Whatever attacked me at night was what was controlling me. And what scared me the most was I didn't know what it was or how to get rid of it.

When the final bell rang, I raced outside into the snow, only to stop dead in my tracks. Where would I go? Why? What was the point? I had to decide. Either move on or end it. Wallowing in despair was no way to live. I turned my face up to the sky and blinked as snow fell lightly on my eyelashes. I wanted to cry out to something, to ask for help or direction, as if there really was a God who could save me, but I held back.

"Hey, bird boy. Looking kinda down." Alex shuffled toward me, eyes half-covered under his winter hat with hands shoved into his pockets. "Why you so sad?"

He was taunting me. I didn't care anymore. I had heard so much the past few weeks from Mitch that simple insults or stabs just washed over me. I was dead to the world.

"Hey. Robin." Alex shoved me as I started walking away. "I'm talking to you."

"So?" I spat and continued on my course away from him.

He grabbed my coat sleeved and yanked me around. "Just stop for a second. I'm trying to…extend a courtesy."

I shook his arm off. "Yeah, well … the last time you *extended one of your courtesies,* it started a whole bunch of things that just made everything worse! So just forget it."

"Don't be so sensitive … here … come here!" Alex grabbed my coat and pulled me closer. "I've got a deal for you." My eyes rested on a tiny bundle of brown powder. I knew exactly what it was. I wanted it.

"So since you're an American, I'm assuming you know what this is," he snarled with a laugh.

"I know what it is! What do you want for it?"

His eyes widened in surprise, and he pulled me over to what I could only assume was an excuse for a shady alley. I looked over my shoulder at the townsfolk bustling around their little country shops, doing their Christmas shopping. None of them had noticed that we had ducked behind the post office. Alex checked around the corners to make sure we were alone before he continued. "So … you want this? It's yours. All you have to do is be available for when our—*supplier* needs something."

I frowned. That wasn't the way it was supposed to work. "What? No—how much does it cost?"

He sighed and checked the perimeter once more. "It's about a hundred dollars a pop, but he doesn't want money."

"He? He who?" I was getting impatient. I was finally looking at something I wanted, and it was just out of my reach.

"Our *supplier.* Look, even I don't know his name. Some bigwig from the city. It's best not to ask too many questions." Alex dangled the bag in front of my nose. "Do you want it or not?"

I grabbed it out of his freezing cold fingers and shoved it in my pocket. "What does he get in return then?"

Alex grinned. "Your … services."

My knees locked, and my head screamed at me to give the drugs back as I started to understand what Alex meant. "You mean, I'd owe him?" If there was one thing I had learned about drug lords in Miami, it was *never, never, ever* owe them anything.

"Yeah, but it's no big deal. He never calls in favours. He just likes to know there's someone there if he needs them. Besides, if he does call it in, me or one of the other guys will go."

Every logical bone in my body that had not been broken of its reason knew it was foolish to agree, but my ache for relief was too strong. I nodded in agreement and darted out of the alley. The police were sitting in their car across the street, and I caught George's eye. He looked at me, and then his gaze shifted to Alex, who was walking in the opposite direction. He knew what had just happened, but he did nothing. Probably as to not get Bret involved. I wasn't going to waste my opportunity, so I took off running. A new force drove me now.

As soon as I got in the barn, I kicked off my outdoor clothing and scampered up the ladder. "Israel?" I called. No answer. Perfect. I sat on my bed cross-legged and anxious and placed the little plastic bundle of brown powder on the blanket in front of me. Never had I imagined I'd get my hands on quality heroin. You never wanted to get involved with that in Miami if you wanted to stay alive. But here in a Podunk little town in the middle of a frozen wasteland? People practically giving it to you for free? I knew what it was, and I knew what it did. It was the only thing that would give me comfort from my pain.

I had never done it before, but I'd seen it done. I knew what to do. I untied the little package and pinched a few grains between my fingers. Without hesitating, I shoved it up my nose and inhaled sharply. A burst of pleasure exploded in my stomach, spreading quickly throughout the rest of my body with tingling sensations. I wanted to laugh in joy at the warmth and comfort that I immediately felt. Everything was not as bad as it once had seemed. I wrapped up the bag of my relief, shoved it under my bed, and looked around the room for something to do. I cleaned, organized, and made my bed. Yeah. I did. Then I took some more heroin. And about fifteen minutes later, I took some more. I have no idea what I did the rest of that day, but I do know this. I thought my dead zone would be over. It had only just begun.

HOLIDAZE

"You seem to be in a relatively good mood lately, Robin. What's up?" Israel sauntered over to me, cup of steaming hot cider in his hand.

It took me a few moments to focus on him and decipher his words. I was too high to answer right away. "Uh … nothing. It's just nice to be out of school, I guess." I attempted a smile and shoved my hands in my pockets. I had no idea if I was good at lying while doped up. The only thing I did know was that I never would have made it on my own. Christmas Eve with the townsfolk couldn't have been more torturous. It was at Eli and Martha's house because theirs was the biggest, and Martha made the best food.

Israel started talking with an elderly couple from the church, and I headed over to the windowsill covered in red candles to watch the snow fall outside. Caleb, the twins, and their friends were running around in the vast sea of white enclosed by the vast sea of dark night. Their shrill laughter and high-pitched shrieks made me long for the days when I could run around on the street with my friends and play ball without a care in the world. If only they knew that their innocent time was coming to an end. Fortunately, the familiar, expected stab of pain in my gut from thinking about the past was suppressed, thanks to Alex and his little bag of heaven. I felt someone next to me.

"Hey there, Robin. How are you?" Lynnette said cheerily, her familiar sunglasses on top of her blonde head replaced with a black hair band. She was wearing a particularly flattering red silk shirt. I hoped my eyes didn't widen.

"Oh yeah … hey, Lynnette. How's things?" I muttered, quickly turning my eyes back to the spectacle outside. She didn't even notice that I didn't answer her question of how I was doing. She chattered away, and I didn't mind. Most of her words bounced off my ears anyway. She was a nice enough girl; I just didn't have anything to say. Most of the evening was like that. People I knew came up to me and talked at me for a few minutes, thinking I was actually paying attention to them just because I periodically nodded my head. Strangers came up and introduced themselves and then promptly remained strangers after they left. Grandpa Joe stared at me a lot. He made me nervous.

However, despite all the distraction, the one thing that occupied my mind the most was when I could get away and get my next fix. Just a few short years ago, I would have been appalled at how quickly I got addicted to drugs, as I had been so adamant about avoiding that scene. But there, at that moment, in that year, nothing else seemed even close to how perfect it was. The euphoric rush, the sensation of flying, the immediate relief … they all seemed too good to be true, especially since I got them for free. I tried not to think about what kind of person I had indebted myself to.

Peter slapped me on the back and beamed out from under his baseball cap. "Hey, Rob. How's it going?"

"Oh, pretty fine. You?"

"Good. Hey, you wanna play some guitar? I brought mine, and one of the other guys brought his."

I definitely wanted to. "Sure … uh, just gimme a sec."

He grinned loudly. "Yeah … I'll be over here tuning."

I made my way out of the living room and to the bathroom. My fingers trembled in excitement as I reached for the tiny bag hidden deep inside my pocket. All traces of fear and anxiety and anything else you can think of disappeared as soon as I fed my cravings. I think I actually laughed out loud. I hadn't laughed in ... well ... a long time. I concealed the bag and darted back to the living room, where Peter was waiting with a beautiful guitar just for me to play on. It was a Taylor, a 1400 series. I had seen one before, but I had never had the chance to play on it.

I sat down on the sofa across from Peter and strummed ever so lightly with my fingertips, for fear of damaging it. It came alive in my hands, adding to my already dream-like state of mind. I'm assuming I played Christmas songs. I'm assuming Peter played with me. I'm assuming a lot of people liked it. I'm assuming everything went fine, everyone left, and I went back to my room to go to sleep. I still can't remember what happened that Christmas Eve. If only I would have known that was just the beginning of not remembering things. I've said that a lot haven't I? If only. My world is built on "if onlys."

"Robin ... hey, Rob ... wake up," Israel cooed and shook me gently as I slept. "It's Christmas."

"So?" I mumbled. As soon as I spoke, I had officially left my dream world; my dream world where everything was happy and fun, and where I didn't feel like my insides were debating whether to destroy themselves or come up and out of my throat. I tried to lay as still as possible.

He shook me again. "Come on ... we're going to open presents."

"Don't!" I croaked. "Don't touch me ..." His fingers had lightly gripped my skin, and it felt like he was sliding a grater down my arm.

Israel knew I would never snap at him like that anymore. He knew I respected him. He knew something was wrong. His voice dropped low. "What's wrong?"

"I don't know," I whispered, trying not to move. I couldn't tell him the truth, and it scared me to death. This was one of those moments where everything could have changed, but it didn't.

"Are you sure?"

I groaned, hoping he'd take it as a yes.

"Well...I guess just sleep. Um...the kids are pretty anxious..."

"Just—go ahead without me." I groaned again and swallowed back something that wanted to come out.

"I'll be back to check on you after." The tone of Israel's voice comforted me. It was how my mom had sounded when I was sick. Sympathetic, sad, willing, and somewhat helpless.

Israel had told me he loved me like a brother, and in turn I had grown to love him back for who he was and what he said and did. His very being demanded respect. I didn't respect Eli because Eli was like every other adult I had ever met: a totally judgmental, close-minded person who just gave up on me. But I respected Israel, like I respected Grandpa Joe. It was because they stood up to me, rebuked me, and took the time to understand me. I even respected little Caleb for the incredible mercy he had shown me. I wished I could tell Israel that I had found something that eased my pain, but I knew he'd disapprove, and if he disapproved, I'd have to give it up. No way was I willing to do that.

At the moment though, the pain that had once been eased had returned full force, along with everything else you can think of. Nausea, headache, dizziness, cramps, everything. I barely made it to the sink, where I heaved my guts out. Shutting my eyes, I turned the water on and let it drain down the sink. I couldn't look at it or it would make me sick again. The rancid smell was enough to keep my stomach turning. I rinsed out my mouth and stumbled back to my bed. My hands groped for my headphones in the drawer by my bed. I needed to disappear, and I didn't have any heroin left. Shoving the hard metal band down on my head, I groaned and turned the volume up as loud as it would go.

Maybe I should just stop this heroin thing. If it makes me this sick without it, is it really worth it? How am I gonna get more? I won't see Alex for another three weeks! How will I survive this?

My mind raced as I tried to block out the sickness with my

music, but it didn't work. In a few minutes, I was hurling into the sink again. I stared in the mirror at my shaky, pale, sick frame.

Why is this happening? How can I still be here? Does God really hate me so much?

"Robin? Are you okay?" Israel's head appeared at the ladder.

I wanted to run to him and cry, but he couldn't know what I had done. He couldn't know about the drugs. "I'm just not doing so well," I replied, my voice breaking as many times as it possibly could.

He walked to me and took my frail arms in his hands. "You look like death," he said, his brow creased with worry. "What's going on?"

I wanted to scream it out, confess it all, and I almost did, until I was taken over. "Nothing!" I snapped, pulling away. "Get away from me!" My voice was low and scratchy; in other words, not mine.

"Robin, you can trust me."

I fought myself. I suppressed it. I regained control. "I'm ... sorry. I didn't mean to. I'm just ... "

Israel put up his hands to stop me. "It's fine. Don't worry about it. Maybe you should sleep some more." He ran his fingers through his newly cut Christmas hair and tried to smile at me. "I'll check on you again."

As soon as Israel left, a searing hot pain stabbed through my stomach.

Don't repress me.

I swore. "Who *are* you?" I gasped through the pain.

I am you.

I stumbled over the clothes on the floor and tried to regain my balance. "No! You're not me! Get away! *I* am me! *I* am me!" I threw myself on my bed and clamped my hands over my ears. What was it? What was talking to me? What was making me say things I didn't want to say? What was taking away my will?

I know where Alex lives.

The pain disappeared. I laid still, my heart racing, my mind repeating those hopeful words.

I know where Alex lives.

I gathered up every ounce of strength in my body and sat up. I needed Alex. I needed what he could offer. I needed to dull the pain. If I never ran out, I would never feel sick again. At that moment, I felt like I had left my body, and I was watching myself put on my coat and boots and run out of the barn.

Somehow, twenty minutes later, frozen and exhausted, I ended up in front of a little brown house with a rusty green pickup truck in the driveway. I re-entered my body and walked up to the front door. I banged on it hard with my fist. The knots in my stomach only got tighter the longer I stood in the cold waiting for someone to answer the door. How did I end up there? Whose house was it? Alex's face appeared in the side window.

"Robin Cane ... what a surprise. I knew I could count on you. Come on in."

"No," I spat, "just gimme another bag."

He leaned against the doorframe and crossed his arms. "Oooh. Feeling tough now, huh?"

"Alex, just gimme some or I'm ratting you out to George."

His mocking grin melted from his face. "Fine. Wait here." He slammed the door in my face. The thought of how I would have to pay for it crossed my mind for a second, but then it was replaced by the sheer desire for it. "Here," Alex said, opening the door and thrusting a paper bag into my chest. "That should be a few weeks in there. I'll probably call on you after that time. You know ... the favour."

I was already halfway down his driveway. "Whatever," I yelled. All I wanted was the safety of my room where I could get my fix and everything would be perfect. If I was lucky, I'd be dead by the time he'd call in the favour.

I AM NOT MY OWN

"Aww … that's not fair," Esther whined as she landed on one of my hotels. Yes, I was playing Monopoly. Somehow, when your senses are dulled, squeaky girls aren't as annoying as usual.

I grinned and leaned back in my chair as she picked which properties to mortgage. That Sunday afternoon wasn't so bad. It was the second Sunday after New Year's. I slept in, got high, and got fed when the fam came home from church. The kids had roped me into playing Monopoly with them, and I was feeling too good and too bored to refuse.

"Don't be a poor loser, Esther," Caleb chimed. He was such a patronizing know-it-all sometimes. Why did he have to be so perfect all the time?

"Shut up, Caleb. I seem to remember a pout on your pretty face when *you* landed in this exact spot!" Esther thrust a wad of fake money at me and pouted for the rest of the game. It lasted only a few minutes more until it was just Israel and I. My mind started to blank and fizz, so he won. I needed to get away for my next fix. At first, I thought I would just take it when I was hurting, but it turned into something more. I needed it all the time. I felt like crap without it. As the kids put the game away, I felt Israel's eyes on me. What was he looking at?

"Hey … Robin … you okay?" he asked, his eyes probing.

"Ch—yeah…why wouldn't I be?" I glared and stood up, too fast. I stumbled into the sofa as the world went black. He grabbed my arm and steadied me. I laughed. Everyone looked at me. I guess they had never heard me laugh before. "What?" I said, struggling to focus. My muscles shook as they rebalanced.

"You don't look so great." Israel kept a firm grip on my arm as I started to walk out of the room. "Maybe you should lie down."

"Maybe you should mind your own business," I seethed. Israel let go and said nothing. I didn't want to snap at him; it just sort of happened. The kids' attention had already shifted. They were scrambling into their outdoor clothes to go play outside.

"Thanks for playing, Robin," the girls said. Caleb looked at me and smiled his saintly smile before bolting out the door after them. I was left alone in the kitchen with Israel, who wasn't looking at me, and wasn't smiling. I felt so guilty. I needed to apologize. I wanted to apologize, but I had no clue where to start. I hadn't apologized since I was twelve.

"Uh…" I began. Israel looked up. "So…I didn't really mean…" My mind went blank. What could I say to make my awful words go away? Nothing.

Israel's face softened and he came over to me. "Thanks." He took my hand and pulled me into his chest for a bone-crushing hug. I could barely breathe.

"Yeah…" I mumbled. "Sure." I still felt awkward around him. I still felt uncomfortable. I still felt unworthy.

"Youth group tonight, Robin…okay?" Israel said as he ruffled my hair and went to the fridge to pour himself some orange juice.

"Uh…" I pulled on the pieces of my hair after he flattened them. "I don't really want to."

"Peter was asking about you today at church, so I told him I'd bring you tonight whether you wanted to or not."

The stab of pain that had attacked me before reminded me that it was still there. "Actually, Israel…I really, really don't want to go."

Israel shoved his glass into the dishwasher and turned it on. "Too bad ... you're going."

I sulked for the rest of the afternoon. I knew he would make me. I would've been willing to let him drag me to the truck, but I decided not to act like a two-year-old. For once. I got in the passenger seat and squished myself as far into the corner as I could and refused to look at Israel. So much for not acting like a two-year-old.

"Robin, what's your problem? Don't you want any friends? Don't you want out of this ... depressive state?"

"No," I mumbled stupidly. Of course I wanted out. But it would never happen. I didn't know how to get out. There was no way out.

"Oh, Robin ... " Israel sighed as he pulled into the iced-over church parking lot. "I don't know what to do."

"How about leaving me alone?" I hissed, slamming the door shut as I hopped out. I was like a girl, my emotions all up and down.

"Don't be stupid, Robin."

"Don't patronize me."

He sighed again and headed inside. I followed, dreading the people I would find there. My feet started to drag. My stomach started to hurl. My entire body slowed down. Something was stopping me from going inside.

"Well?" Israel coaxed as he held the door open for me.

I seriously couldn't move. I wanted to go in, to make him happy after I had just bit his head off, but I couldn't move.

He sauntered over to me and grabbed my arm, pulling me inside. "Come on ... knock this off. You'll embarrass yourself."

He budged me from my concrete stance and led me inside the glowing warmth of the church that should've been comforting but instead taunted me with incineration.

"Robin! Hey, everyone. Robin came!" Lynnette squealed as she waved at me and tried not to spill her cup of hot cocoa. The room chimed "hello" to me, but I wasn't paying attention. I was paying attention to someone else. Peter was glaring at me. As soon as our eyes met, the stabbing pain returned in my stomach. I tried not to cry out loud as I looked away.

"Hey, pal, it's great you came," Patrick said as he slapped me on the back. My first instinct was to tear out his throat, but the pain was holding me back.

"Robin, what's wrong?" Israel whispered in my ear.

"Nothing," I lied. The truth was I had no idea what was happening. It seemed like I was having an allergic reaction to—the other people in the room. I sat down in the corner and secretly felt my stomach and ribs, hoping to find some kind of bone protruding as a source for the pain. Nothing. A game started, but I waved them off and said I'd watch. They didn't care much, so they left me alone in my agony. All but one. Peter continued to watch me. Every time I met his eyes, I felt intoxicated. I leaned my head against the cold glass of the window and focused on forgetting the pain. I wanted my drugs. I needed them. The desire was so strong I could already taste them.

Leave … leave now.

My eyes shot open.

"Okay, guys, time to settle down." Patrick was taking his seat in the middle of the room. "Come on and sit." Everyone congregated in front and around. I was still left out of the circle, thank goodness. "So the topic I had prepared for tonight…" Patrick began.

Get out.

I wanted to panic. I was hearing a voice, and it wasn't my conscience

"…something else has been placed on my mind. I wanted to remind you all what our Lord has done for us." Patrick flipped open his Bible and kept talking.

My eyes would not focus on his face no matter how hard I tried.

"God—what an awesome God is he. He created us in his image so we might have a relationship with him. But sin came into the world, and foolishly we fell away. But he sought after us. Chased us!"

My heart started to pound out of my chest. Why did I have to fight to hear what he was saying?

"Think of it this way. A father, a landowner, has a wonderful, loyal son. He also has a servant who stole from him, lied to him, and tried to run away from him. For all of which, the penalty was death." Patrick swallowed and continued. Sweat was forming on his brow. "The father says to his son, 'Son, I love you, but I love my servant too. Would you die in his place so that he may be washed clean of his guilt?'"

My heart cried out. I wanted to hear this. This was important, I knew it, but my eyes wouldn't stay focused.

"The son died in the wicked servant's place, because the father loved the servant so much. That is what God did for us."

I stood. I don't know why. Suddenly I was standing.

"There is nothing we can do that will separate us from the love that is in Christ."

"That's a lie!" I heard a voice say. I thought I was the only one who could hear it, but I realized soon that was not the case. Everyone turned to look at me, horror on their faces. I had said those words. My eyes blacked out. I don't know what happened. I found myself standing back at the window, watching Peter come toward me.

"Robin," he stretched out his hand, "can I pray for you?"

"No!" I spat. My eyes focused again, and I looked at him with as much hatred as I could.

Patrick appeared behind him. "Robin, is there anything you would like to talk about?"

I was being threatened. I backed away and pressed up against the wall. "Get away from me," my scratchy voice said. The kids in the room all immediately closed their eyes. They started praying.

Peter and Patrick looked at each other. I wish I could've known what they were thinking. "Come on, Robin, maybe we should pray." Peter reached out and gently took my arm. He might've thought he was being gentle, but it felt like he had just grabbed me with a thousand knives. I screamed and jerked away from him.

"What are you doing?" Israel yelled, and he took me in his arms. His arms didn't hurt me.

Peter took off his baseball cap, and Patrick said something in a harsh whisper to Israel, but I didn't care what it was. I wanted to go home. Get away from all the shocked faces. I wanted to see how much damage Peter had inflicted on my arm. I thought we were going to go. I thought that Israel was on my side, but his grip on me tightened. My skin started to burn where he was touching me. I frantically looked around at the faces of the three who crowded me. Israel held me from behind, not letting my arms go. Patrick took my head in his hands, and Peter took hold of my shoulder. Bubbles of fire erupted from underneath my skin. A bloodcurdling scream filled the youth room as Patrick, Israel, and Peter prayed for me. They let go, and I fell to my knees. I looked up at their faces. While they had been holding me, their faces were evil, contorted, and disfigured. But they had returned to normal, and my body was no longer on fire.

"What—what did you do to me?" I asked, my shaky but normal voice had returned.

Peter and Patrick just watched me, their faces focused and their chests heaving.

Israel lifted me up and steered me toward the exit. "Come on. We're going home. I'll explain."

I let Israel lead me outside to the truck while watching the exhausted and worried expressions of the people we left behind. As we were driving back, I looked at Israel for some kind of sign or clue as to what was going on, but he looked even more confused than I felt. I wanted to sink into a hole in the ground and fall forever. What was happening to me? Was I going crazy? Was I losing my mind? As I thought about the prayers Peter and Patrick had said for me, my head felt free and light, but after only a minute or so, my chest caved in. The fire inside my stomach returned. I looked at my arm where Peter had grabbed me. Flesh was hanging from it, blood gushing. I could see the bone.

"Oh … my …" I moaned.

Israel looked at me frantically. "What?"

My wails filled the cab as I squirmed, my lifeless arm lying on my lap. I yelled his name. I screamed for him to help me.

He pulled the truck over to the side of the road and reached for my face. "Robin! Tell me!"

I strained my eyes as far away from my shredded arm as they would go, my voice sputtering out its last sounds. "H … elp …"

Israel's hands were wrapped around my head and face. "I can't if you don't tell me what's wrong."

"My … arm …" I croaked, forcing myself to look down.

"There's nothing wrong with your arm, Robin."

I looked. No blood. No bone. "What?" I croaked. I felt it with my hand. Nothing hurt.

Israel turned my face to look at his. "Robin, you're scaring me."

I swallowed and shivered. "I'm … scaring myself." I pushed his hands away. "Can you just drive?" I looked at my arm one last time before pressing on my temples. What had I seen? Was I dreaming? I tried to picture what I had seen my arm look like, but it was just a blur. I needed my drugs. I needed them bad. But I couldn't get them.

Israel didn't leave my side for one second. He got me up to the room and stuck me in bed. I know he sat there, his ears perfectly tuned to every noise I made. I couldn't get my fix. I could feel it starting. The shakiness. The panic rushing deep inside my body. The nausea creeping up. I lay deathly still in the dark, my own ears strained for the sound of Israel's breathing. I waited until I was absolutely sure before I reached under my bed for the small plastic bag. You have no idea how amazing it was to finally satisfy the need. My panic went away, the nasty thoughts and feelings. I was floating. I was fine. I was sleeping peacefully. I didn't know that I owed my serenity not to the heroin, but to Israel, who stayed up the entire night praying fervently that the demons would leave me alone.

KICKED OUT

"So how was youth group last night, boys?" Eli asked, immersed in his newspaper.

I looked over at Israel. I couldn't remember much of what had happened, but I did remember that it was far from a good experience. My evil disposition had taken over; I knew that. What I did and why was what I couldn't remember. I hoped I didn't embarrass myself.

"It was fine, Dad," Israel lied.

Eli didn't even look at me. I wondered if he would hate me forever. And he didn't even know what I was really doing!

"Come on, Robin, let's go. I'll walk you to school." Israel stood up from the breakfast table, and I followed.

"Thanks for breakfast, Martha," I said quietly, hoping maybe it might make her not hate me as much.

She looked up at me, her eyes softening. "You're welcome, Robin. Be good at school."

My heart warmed a little. "Okay." I put on my coat and grabbed my stupid red bag. Man, I hated that bag.

"So…" Israel began as we walked down the snow-covered driveway.

"So?" I looked at him and tried not to stare in shock. I had never seen anyone so exhausted. It surprised me he was even standing. "You don't look so good."

He nodded grimly and sniffed. "I'm not feeling too good."

"Why?"

"Rough night."

Oh no. He saw me. He was watching. I'm dead.

"Robin?"

"What?" I squeaked out, trying to act as if nothing was wrong.

"I was wondering what you thought of youth group last night—what Patrick spoke about."

All of a sudden, the memories came flooding back. I had to fight to keep from drowning in it. "Uh … I … don't know." What had I said? Had I screamed at them? Why? I remembered what Patrick had said about God loving us so much that he let his son die, but I also remembered that while he was speaking, something inside me was trying to inflict as much pain as possible. Something inside me didn't want me listening to Patrick speak.

"Everything he said was true. God does love you that much."

"Well, I've already figured all that out so … " I kicked at some snow to try to avoid the awkwardness.

"So what do you think?"

The icy, mid-January winter air started to creep up the front of my coat. I shivered and tried to clear my mind to set Israel straight once and for all. "Sure, maybe there is a creator, but he doesn't care about me. No one who really cared would stand by and—watch while *things* happen."

"But that's not what he does, Robin. He doesn't just stand by idly. He's waiting for you to come to him so he can—"

"Oh, so it's all on me, huh?"

"That's not—"

"You know what, Israel?" I interrupted again. "God doesn't care about me! He couldn't possibly! And what if I did pray? What would he do? Bring my mom back? Kill me? Both of the options that would make me happy are impossible! So why bother?" My chest heaved as it tried to catch up with me. The school was in sight, and I made a bolt for it, except that Israel caught me and held me back. His tired eyes, distraught and pleading as he held me close.

"Robin, don't you understand what's happening to you?"

"What? What is happening to me?" I challenged.

"Satan is taking a hold of you. He's trying to control you." Israel's hands tightened on my arms.

A stab of fear overcame the usual stab of pain for a moment. "What?"

"He's inside you, Robin. Last night...I saw them hovering over your bed."

I was either shivering from standing in the snow, or I was shaking in terror. "You saw *what* over me?"

"You know, don't you? You can hear him," Israel whispered.

Of course I knew. The voice. The controlling force. I had never put all the pieces together before. I tightened my grip on Israel's coat sleeves, suddenly feeling awake and vulnerable. "It hurts me."

"I know. We have to—"

"No!" I yelled. The few seconds I had alone with myself were gone. I could feel the anger welling up inside again. "Don't talk about it. Just...I'll be fine." I broke away from him and started toward school.

"Robin, please!" Israel called.

I ignored him. The very idea was ridiculous. It was the heroin, that's what was making me sick. The voice—only a hallucination. I could deal with it.

What a load of crap, I thought. *He saw them hovering over me? What did that even mean? Stupid.*

I made my way into biology late. Peter wasn't there.

Yes... that's right. It's only the drugs. Everything's fine.

That's what my mind said, but I knew everything wasn't fine. I was in deep trouble, and there was no way out. The whole day was like that. I forced myself to believe my own lie. Right before my last class, I stole away into the bathroom for another dose. I needed it so badly. I practically shoved the doors open and ran over a few other students, who hastily scrambled out of my way. The anticipation of the peace and respite I would soon feel was intense. My fingers clumsily fumbled with the little bag as I checked over my shoulder to make sure no one had come in. As soon as I had shoved it up my nose, I waited for the feeling to come. It came, but in a different way. My nose itched, and no matter of scratching could satisfy it. The blood rushing faster and faster through my body felt like it had caught on fire. I tried to stabilize myself against the grimy sink.

What's wrong? Something's wrong! Why am I feeling like this?

The bathroom door opened. It was Mitch.

"Oh, hey there, Miami. Still alive?"

I didn't even think. I lunged myself at him and ploughed him into the wall. Since I had caught him by surprise, he never had a chance to defend himself. I punched and kicked, and as soon as he was down, I smashed his head into the floor as many times as I could. Someone eventually pulled me off him, but I don't know who. All I know is that I eventually ended up in the principal's office with blood on my hands, and my head swimming in its own surreal world.

"Mr. Cane," the well-dressed principal began, "I am aware of your ... unfortunate situation, but I am afraid I cannot be extending you any more special courtesies."

I knew what he was saying, but I couldn't make myself respond.

"You are failing every class, Mr. Cane. Did you know that?"

The fire in my blood was cooling. My eyelids were falling heavy and fast; the trip I was on was winding down.

"Mr. Cane!"

I jolted. "What?"

"You're grades. They are all Fs. Do you ever plan on fixing that?"

My brain buzzing, I mumbled a sound. I don't know if it was a yes or a no. Honestly, it didn't matter.

"And this ... violent nature. Fighting without cause? Is this ever going to subside?"

"You know what, mister? I seriously can't understand a word you're saying." I laughed.

He glared. He sighed. "I'm afraid that you will no longer be able to attend this school. You are a bad influence on our students, and I cannot take the risk of your volatile nature. This is the third or fourth count of physical violence from you. I refuse to put up with any more."

It took a few moments for me to realize that he had just kicked me out. "Wait … you're … expelling me?"

"Yes."

I let myself out of his office and stumbled toward my locker. I couldn't believe he didn't notice I was doped up. What would I tell Israel? What would Eli say? I was finished in his house for sure. I tugged on my coat and trudged outside, ready to go back to the farm and face the danger, but then a thought came. If I didn't go back, they wouldn't know I had been kicked out. I could just go out every day and get high, and no one would know the difference. I bent down to the ground and picked up a handful of snow. My hands went numb as I rubbed it over the bloodstains on my skin. Somehow, even though the plan I had come up with seemed ideal, I knew it would never last. In a tiny town, everyone knew everyone's business in a matter of hours. I just decided to see how long it would last, and then I'd figure how to deal with Eli's wrath when it finally descended on me.

FREE, BUT NOT WHAT I HAD IN MIND

I screamed as loud as I could. I tugged at the ropes binding me, rubbing my skin raw. The fire licked my face and took off half of my skin. He had set me on fire. The one who haunted me. The one who controlled me. He had set me on fire.

Please! I shouted. *Put it out!* But no one did.

"Stop!"

I heard Israel's voice, and I tried to call out for him, but the fire was in my face, searing my skin. I shook my head and tried to breathe, but the thick smoke filled my nose and mouth.

"Leave him alone, I command you!" Israel bellowed at the top of his lungs. All of a sudden, the ropes were ripped off and the flames died away like someone had sucked all the oxygen out. My mind suddenly became aware of reality. I was bent over the side of my bed, sobbing into the sheets. Israel's grip on my arms was turning my skin black and blue. "Robin, can you hear me?"

I tried to breathe consistently to calm my heart, but panic was surging through every part of my body. My hands flew to my face to see if my skin was still there. "Where ... I need ... " I mumbled and squinted through the tears as I looked for my heroin.

For the last three days, I had been high almost twenty-four-seven, and fortunately, no one from the school had contacted Eli about my expulsion. Things couldn't be more … perfect.

"Robin, what do you need?" Israel's purple face looked at mine. His grip on my bruised arms loosened as he slid onto the bed and sat.

I held onto his hand and tried to get a hold of myself emotionally and physically. Flashes of fire kept popping into my mind. I crammed my eyes shut and forced them to go away. "I need … my … I need … drugs."

"Medicine?" Israel stood up on his wobbly legs and headed to his dresser drawer. "Here. I have some aspirin."

I took the two white pills Israel handed to me and tossed them down my throat.

I fought the evil one. I sat on my bed and I fought him inside. He was there. I could feel him. He was reviving my dormant, mutated heart. The mutated heart that Israel's love had somehow managed to subdue. The voice had always been around, but it had never done this to me before. I had tried to deny its presence, but there was no denying it now.

"Israel…" I croaked. He rushed to sit next to me, his tired eyes wiping themselves of all pain just to focus on mine. "He's inside me. I don't want…"

"Robin, I've been fighting him off for days, but he keeps coming back. Do you know why?"

"No." Tears rolled down my face. He was already starting to hurt me inside.

"Because you have nothing to fill that hole inside you. You have nothing to protect you."

"Well, I don't know what—," I started.

"You need the protection of Jesus! He's been here the whole time just yearning for you to ask him to help you; for you to put your life in his hands."

Searing pain stabbed me in the gut. "Oh…" I moaned. He was fighting for his hold on me.

"Robin, can we pray? We'll get him out and invite Jesus in." Israel's eyes welled with fear and intensity. "Do you believe Jesus can help you?"

"Yes," I sobbed, leaning over from the pain. "Get him out!" Israel prayed. For what seemed like hours. I screamed and cursed at him. I even tried to hit him. But I knew that was just the thing trying to stay inside me. "Pray, Robin! Ask Jesus to fill you with his spirit!" Israel said, struggling to hold onto me.

My mind was a tornado of feelings, visions, and thoughts. I knew what I had to do to get rid of the evil one. I wanted to ask Caleb's Jesus to help me, but it wouldn't let me. I tried. I tried to say it. I could feel the words in my head, I could feel them in my throat, but every time I got close to blurting it out, it would stab me with the pain of my worthlessness; the pain of my failure; the pain of my captivity.

"Come on, Robin! Fight him!" Israel ordered.

I demanded my mind to clear up. I demanded my freedom. *I can do it. Get out of my head! You can't control me! I can do this!*

"Jesus, save me from him!" I screamed. The pain was immediately torn from my body. I could feel it leave me. My chest was light. It was gone.

"Israel?" I trembled.

He grabbed me and held me for a long time, crying out his own exhaustion. "It's going to be okay now. The demon is gone."

My heart almost stopped at the word. Was that what it was? Hadn't Israel mentioned that before? A demon. The demon was the one decaying my soul. The demon was the one controlling my actions and thoughts. Why hadn't I seen it before? Because it had been clouding my vision. The demon had been masquerading as my conscience. But this Jesus … he had defeated him. All I did was call out his name, and he helped me. Maybe this Jesus really was the real deal.

"Israel," I said, sighing out the weight of the world, "I'll be late for school." My mind had immediately averted to what my body craved the most.

Israel wiped his face and ran his fingers through his hair. "Don't be ridiculous. You're not going to school. You are exhausted, and so am I." He stood up and practically face-planted into his bed and fell fast asleep. I sat for a few moments, trying once again to decipher my real reality. I felt free and alive for the first time in years. Jesus, son of God, had saved me from the devil. What could I give him in return?

My trust … I suppose that's where it has to start.

Catching up with what my mind had already remembered, my body suddenly realized that it was lacking something important, and it started to shake. It had been too long since my last dose. I tried to make my spinning mind remember where I had hid my stash.

My red backpack. Where is it?

I surveyed the room. Nothing. I got up and actually moved things, and I even did it without falling over. Still nothing. I threw on some jeans and prepared to make my way to the house, for fear I had left it in there, when I heard the front door slam. I shuffled to the window and looked out. What I saw hit me like a sledgehammer. Eli was storming toward the barn with the red backpack in his hand. I backed away from the window and scrambled to come up with a quick, believable lie, but my mind drew a blank. After what I had just been through, that was not surprising. The familiar fear started to creep back in. I clawed at my sweatshirt collar and tried to control my breathing.

Israel sat up immediately from his deep sleep, and his eyes locked with mine. "Are you okay?"

I flinched as the barn door opened and crashed shut. Eli clomped up the ladder in his big boots. "Israel! Get out!"

Israel scrambled out of his bed and hastily looked between me and the red bag. "Dad, what—"

"Out!" Eli seethed as he threw the backpack at me. I clumsily caught it and pleaded with my eyes for Israel to stay, but he knew better than to cross his father … though I never did hear the barn door open or close.

"Empty it," he ordered.

My shaky hands turned the bag upside down and shook. The

two packets of drugs I had left plopped out onto the floor. I stared at them in shock, almost as if I hadn't known they were there.

"I'm..." Eli spoke in a low, quiet voice. His mouth wavered from his usual straight line. "I'm only going to ask you one question, and I'm only going to ask it once. If you dare lie to me..."

I waited. This was the end. Guilt overwhelmed me as I didn't expect it would.

"Are you on these?" He pointed to the heroin on the floor with a disgusted finger.

I trembled at the answer I knew I had to give. "Yes."

Eli closed his eyes and clenched his hands together. "I see." He turned his back to me. "Out."

I wanted to protest, but none of the words I could think of would ever be enough.

"Get...out," he ordered. "Fifteen minutes, or I call the police." His shadow descending the ladder disappeared in my tears. I turned and blindly started grabbing anything I could get my hands on and shoving it into my duffel that was under the bed.

"Robin..." Israel's voice carried over to my ears.

I continued to stuff, motivated by the thoughts of Bret catching me with drugs, or Eli throwing me off his land physically.

"Robin. Drugs? How could you?"

I spun around and snatched the bags from his sweaty hands. "Because it's the only thing that gives me any relief! It's the only thing that..." I stopped talking and shoved the two bags into my pocket.

"You don't need that now! You have God. He can—"

"He can what, Israel? Save me? Eli's throwing me out! Where am I supposed to go? Does God have a house?" I zipped up my bag and shoved my feet into my Converse, completely forgetting that God had actually just finished saving me.

"Robin, if you say you don't need them...if you stop using...maybe I can convince him to—"

I shook my head and bowled past him. "I can't say that because

I do need them. Besides, I don't need you *religious* people ruling my life." My own words humiliated me. I didn't want to leave. I didn't want to be a slave to drugs. I didn't want demons inside me anymore. But I didn't know what to do. I got outside into the winter air and came face to face with the entire family, arguing.

"Daddy, no! You can't send him away! He needs us!" Caleb screamed through his tears.

Eli shook his son off his arm and headed toward me. "I've made my decision."

Martha stood in the doorway, expressionless but clearly upset, yelling at her girls to stay inside the house.

"Dad, this is *not* right," Israel said as he bolted out of the barn behind me.

"I'll tell you what's not right, Israel!" Eli twisted his ratty cap on his head, his breath billowing in the cold air. "A boy who refuses to cooperate in any way or compromise. A boy who lies, cheats, and steals. A boy who almost killed your little brother, who bullied kids at school, got kicked out, and spent the rest of the time getting high!" Eli's face burned with rage as he reached the spot where I was standing, petrified of the next moments to come.

Israel stepped in between Eli and me. "Dad, Robin is going to try to start over!"

"That's a lie! I see it on his face. He tells you what you want to hear, Israel! He has you wrapped around his finger!" Eli pushed his son aside and grabbed me by the back of the neck. "I've tried everything with you, Robin, and you still refuse to compromise! I cannot, and will not, inflict you on my family any longer!"

I felt the tears of rejection and sorrow try to seep out as he pushed me away from him, hard. I stumbled a few steps and then turned around at the sound of another voice.

"*He* is your family, Elijah." Grandpa Joe went and stood next to Eli. "If you send him away, you're condemning him."

"Oh great, now is the time you decide to speak up, Dad? You barely ever say a word except in *his* defence! Dad, you're wrong. If I *don't* send him away, I condemn him. This is the only way he will learn! Caleb … in the house," Eli yelled once Caleb had started to protest again. He then turned his attention back to me. "Robin, I'm sorry. I've tried. This is the only option I see left." Eli's voice broke as he turned away from me and headed back into his house with Martha. "Israel!" he called, invisible already.

Israel started to head toward me, but Grandpa Joe held him back. "Listen to your father, boy."

Israel looked at me one last time before obeying his grandfather and heading in the house. "Robin, you're not alone. Don't forget."

I nodded and tried to look confident for his sake. He was more scared than I had ever seen him. He ran inside, most likely to argue with Eli some more. My pained eyes rested on Grandpa Joe as he trudged over to me.

"Boy … " his gravelly voice said, "there's an elderly couple over on Wood Street who have a spare bedroom. They'll take you in. We'll figure out what to do from there." He put his rough, wrinkly hand on my head. I tried not to break down as he turned from me and left to join his family inside the warm house. I stood frozen in the snow, staring at the place that held the only family I had in the world, knowing that they didn't want me in their life. I had tried. I had tried so many times and failed. I had tried to hate them, to make it so I wouldn't care. I had tried to kill myself, to make it so they wouldn't have to care. I had tried to block the pain with drugs, and all that accomplished was isolating me completely. The only thing that showed any promise at all was God. He had defeated the demon, and even though I was cast out from my family, maybe he was still there. I didn't want to think about what it would have been like to have been cast out *and* have something evil controlling me.

I turned and headed down the icy gravel road—Wood Street my destination with resolve—but despair soon overwhelmed me, and I was sobbing my heart out. If there was ever a time where I was lost, it was then.

THE WORST DECISION EVER

"Hey, Cane! Is that you?"

I looked up from my lap and stared at Alex. Once I had gotten to Wood Street, I realized I had no idea which house the couple lived in, or even what their names were. I had sat down on a bench, completely and utterly at a loss. Again. "Yeah, Alex, it's me."

"How you doin'?" he said, sitting down next to me.

I scoffed and tried to sink deeper into my coat. "Eli kicked me out."

"Ah ... found 'em, didn't he?"

I nodded in shame. How could things have possibly gotten so bad?

"Bro, don't worry about it. You can crash with me." Alex smiled and pushed his hat up out of his eyes. "Besides, this is perfect. Now you won't have them breathing down your neck about this weekend." He stood up and grabbed my duffel.

"What's this weekend?" I asked as I followed him down the street I had been pacing.

Alex turned to me and flashed me a strange smile that was mixed with dread. "The boss called in the favour."

I stayed silent until we got to his house. He told me he lived with his mom, but I didn't see her anywhere. Single mom, probably working all the time to put food on the table. It was a tiny place, but it was clean, and Alex had the entire basement to himself for a room. It was better than my loft with Israel, at least that's what I told myself so I wouldn't start crying again.

"You can bunk there." He threw my bag onto an overstuffed couch in the corner under the window. I sat down, somewhat astounded that I had a place to stay, as I was preparing to sleep on the streets that night. He plopped on his bed and threw his hat on the floor. Ruffling his hair, he smiled. It was strange for me, thinking that Alex was now the only friend I had. When I had met him, I knew he was the wrong crowd, and I hated him, but it's amazing who becomes your friend when you are desperate.

"Uh ... thanks," I mumbled. "I guess I'd be ... "

"Dying in the snow right now? Yeah, I know." Alex laughed again and kicked off his shoes. "You know, Cane ... you really are an interesting thing."

"And why is that?" I took my own coat off and lay down on the incredibly comfortable couch.

"I hate you—I think you know. But you are going to save me."

"What are you talking about?" My eyelids were drooping. I realized I probably hadn't slept at all the night before.

Alex got quiet. I looked up because he never got quiet. His mocking face turned serious as he looked at me. "Last time I went to pay him back, he didn't ... approve. So I'm in debt, big time. But fortunately for me, you are exactly what he's been looking for."

I was confused. "What does that even mean?" Sitting up, I began to lose the small sense of comfort Alex's basement was offering me. "What kind of favours are these anyway? I'm not killing anyone, Alex!"

Alex's easy-going smile came back as he put his headphones on. "It's not murder, Robin. Geez, what kind of person do you think I am? Just relax. Take a nap. My mom will cook for us when she gets home."

"Whatever," I whispered, falling back onto the couch. I was too worn out to worry about every little thing. There was one thing I did know, and that was no one was going to make me do anything I didn't want to do. They could threaten me all they wanted, but just like before, I wasn't afraid of death. But I welcomed it.

I slept for a long time, and it was one of the better sleeps I had ever had. There was no one in my head polluting my thoughts or screwing with my feelings. When I woke up, I thanked this Jesus person for keeping the demons away.

"Wake up, Miami," Alex said as he threw a small pizza box at me. "Mom came home late, so she brought pizza." Someone else was with him.

"How you doing?" River asked, not really wanting to know but only asking for lack of a better greeting. I nodded meekly and turned to the food I was handed. Having not eaten all day, I was feeling the hunger pains. I stuffed it down, not paying attention to what River and Alex were talking about. I wish I had been paying attention, but instead, my mind wandered to Israel. I wondered what he was doing. I wondered if he was still trying to get Eli to change his mind. Maybe I would only have to stay with Alex one night, and then the next day they would come for me and give me another chance.

A woman in a short leather skirt and a tight pink sweater came down the stairs with a pizza box and a case of beer. "Lexi, baby? Do you have enough pizza down here?"

"Mom! Not now…just, give me that and go back upstairs." Alex grabbed the food from her and scowled as best as he could. She didn't leave.

"Oh! You're that kid who tried to kill the little Neufeldt boy?" She turned to me with her glittered eyes and put her hands on her hips. "Bet they kicked you out then? So would I."

I tried to hide my guilt as I looked away. I couldn't stand any more condemnation.

"Tell me," she leaned over me, her perfume making me sick, "is my son in danger?"

"Mom!" Alex yelled. "Get out of here."

She smirked at me and left. I wanted to die right then and there. The pizza I had just stuffed down my throat started to rise.

"Sorry, bro. Sometimes she doesn't know when to shut up," Alex said as he sat down on a chair in front of me. "Forget it."

I couldn't forget. I'd never forget.

"Alex. Come on. I got it." River tossed his empty beer can on the floor and opened up his backpack.

"Sweet!" Alex bounded up. "You so owe me this after last time."

"Yeah, I know. Here … you first." River handed Alex a black bundle. A plastic cord was hanging out of it.

"What are you guys doing?" I asked quietly. I knew what it was; I had just never seen it before.

"What does it look like, Miami?" Alex said as he tied his arm off with the cord. I watched him as he mixed heroin with water into an ordinary kitchen spoon and held it over a lighter. Then he filled a syringe up and injected the mix into his vein; his eyes rolled to the back of his head, and he slumped back on his pillow. I wanted it. I wanted it so badly it hurt. Alex's face was so serene it made me realize even more how horribly depressed and dejected I was.

River knew I was eyeing it. He took the bundle from Alex's limp hands and came to sit next to me. "You want this, Robin?" He held it out to me, and I knew this was another one of those "point of no return" moments. I started to shake my head no, but then I realized I had nothing to lose. There was no way Eli would give me another chance. Maybe this would be my chance. If it didn't make me feel better, it would kill me.

"Yes," my voice cracked out.

His dark eyes narrowed as he leaned in closer to my face. "You must be positive before you do this. You do this and everything changes. Do you understand?"

I didn't. I looked over at Alex and envied the amazing time he seemed to be having, and at that moment I would've given anything to feel as he felt. "Yeah, I get it." I held out my arm.

River set to work, his long black hair falling into his face as he bent over. I watched every movement he made and every step he took to prepare the drug and the needle. My heart raced as he tied my arm off swiftly and tightly, not hesitating for a second. He poked at my arm a bit with his fingers before looking at me and saying, "See you on the other side." The needle pierced my skin, and the freezing hot liquid rushed into my vein. It was as if I burst into the air and flew at a million miles an hour. I wish I could describe it better, but there really aren't words. Everything happened at once, better than it had happened before. Vibrant colors filled my eyes as I flew higher and higher, leaving everything bad behind me. I saw my mom and my dad. I saw Justin and Israel. I smiled at them, and joy took hold of me. But then I stopped flying and I started falling. Everything turned to dust and fire. I was back in Alex's room. I heard laughter as I threw up all over myself and the couch. I think my last thought was, "It was worth it," but for the life of me, I can't even begin to imagine where I would come up with that ridiculous idea.

CITY OF HORROR

"Wake up, Miami. We leave in ten minutes."

I forced my eyes open the third time Alex yelled at me. My body ached as I sat and stretched.

"You look like crap. Take a shower or something." Alex threw me a towel. "Come on ... hurry up."

I stumbled toward the bathroom, not having a clue what time it was or what I was doing. Somehow, I managed to successfully take a shower and fix my hair, in which I could see the blond roots again. Dang it. I did enjoy its new length, though. It almost touched my shoulders in certain places it had grown so long. I couldn't remember the last time I had a haircut.

"Miami!" Alex yelled through the door. "River's here with the car!"

"Yeah, yeah," I mumbled, digging for my drugs. As soon as I had my dose, I was able to focus a little better. Ironic, isn't it? We were going into the city to pay our supplier, the boss, and apparently I owed a lot, counting all the bags I had gotten from Alex for free and the last four hits River had given me. I reapplied my eyeliner as I tried to be satisfied with the heroin I had just snorted instead of an injection, but I knew what I wanted. I wanted mainline or nothing.

"Cane!" Alex pounded on the door.

"Relax!" I yelled as I opened it in his face. "I'm here!"

He threw my coat at me and led the way outside to the car, swearing. "If we're late, we're in trouble."

I still had no idea what we were going to do for him. They wouldn't tell me. I knew what it was though. It would be stealing cars, sneaking drugs past cops, or finding some guy and beating him down for cash that he owed. I didn't really care. I just didn't want it to be killing anyone, and as long as it wasn't that, I'd do probably anything for my relief. We drove for about an hour, the last few minutes of that weaving our way through four-lane traffic and bright city lights. The south side of Edmonton reminded me of Miami, except a little more ... backwoods.

"Where are we going?" I asked, still annoyed that I didn't know anything.

"White Avenue. Now shut up," snapped River. He confused me. He was so quiet and reserved, but he just exerted authority, and of course, fear. We pulled up to the side of the road and Alex got out of the front seat. "Get out," River ordered. "I'll come once I've parked."

I obeyed and followed Alex inside a rundown apartment building through the back entrance. I felt extremely uneasy as we entered the little lobby. It looked as if it used to be a hotel but they had shut it down because it didn't pass health inspection. "Hey, D!" Alex yelled.

A short black man poked his head out of the other room. "Hey, Alex. Whut up, sweetie?"

"Tell the boss I brought him."

D took a look at me and nodded his head, disappearing once more.

"Now we wait," Alex said. "Just be quiet."

Two other boys were standing off in a corner, looking sullen and tired. One was staring at the clock on the wall, and the other one was staring at his shoes. They were no older than me. The stuffy heat of the tiny room was getting to me, so I unzipped my coat and tried to relax. River eventually came in the door, brushed right by me, and headed down the hallway. Alex told him "good luck," but he didn't respond. I guessed he was doing his own thing. I hoped I wasn't going to be left alone.

"Alex, what is this?" I looked at him for an answer, expecting him to tell me to shut up, but he didn't say anything. He just stared straight ahead, more anxious than I had ever seen him. My fear started to rise in my throat. I was so tired of being afraid.

D came back and pointed to both Alex and me. Alex pushed me forward, and we followed the little man down the hallway. *Good*, I thought, *at least I'm with Alex.* My reassuring thought was immediately proven irrelevant.

D opened a door on the left, and Alex pushed me through it. Alone. "Alex? You're not coming in?"

He avoided my gaze. "I'm in the room across the hall," he said stoically as he left and D shut the door. I heard him lock it. I tried the door handle, but it didn't move.

"What the crap is this?" I muttered to myself. I heard someone clear a throat behind me. I turned around and saw him, just sitting, watching me.

"Hello," the man in the expensive grey suit said.

I pressed into the door as far as I could. "Who are you?" my timid voice ventured.

"My name is Benton. What is your name?" he said, rising from his seat and coming toward me.

I don't know why I told him, "Robin."

"Robin. That's a nice name." As he came closer and closer to me, I knew exactly what it was he wanted; what I was expected to give him. If this was the "favour," I would rather die.

"Don't touch me," I said to him.

Benton smiled a disturbing smile. He was inches from me. "I'm not going to hurt you, Robin. I've been waiting for someone like you." He reached out and touched my hair. "I like your hair. It's beautiful."

My stomach wrenched into a million knots as he scanned my body with his eyes. His head started to move in closer to mine. On instinct, I reached up and punched him in the face.

"Why you little—," he swore as he stumbled back and wiped

blood from his lip. I knew it was coming, so I closed my eyes. My cheek felt like it split in two as he backhanded me. I fell onto the small table that sat by the door, blackness blotting out my eyes. He grabbed the back of my shirt and dragged me toward the middle of the room. I had been so terrified of him I hadn't even noticed that the only thing in the room was a bed. He threw me on the smelly mattress, and my adrenaline kicked in. I rolled off and tried to get around him and get to the door. He blocked me every time.

"What are you doing? I paid big money for this!" he fussed.

"Then you need a refund, you fag!" I screamed, trying to sound tough. I thought I had felt fear before, but when he ran at me and tackled me to the ground, everything in me panicked to the point of hyperventilation.

"I see. You're playing hard to get. Creative."

A dry sob escaped my throat as he started to play with the collar of my shirt, his fingernails scratching my neck. "Be quiet," he soothed as his hands started to travel downwards.

I did the only thing I could think of. I grabbed him where it would hurt and twisted as hard as I could. His scream of bloody murder assured me I had succeeded. I pushed with all my might and got him off me. Scrambling to my feet, I heard him moaning behind me, trying to follow. I grabbed the door handle and yanked. It wouldn't budge, but like I said before, when you're desperate and your adrenaline kicks in...

I bashed the door with all my strength. I kicked at it until I broke it. Screaming Alex's name, I hastily looked behind me to see if Benton had made it up off the floor. He had. The door right across the hall opened and Alex appeared inside it. He didn't have his shirt on.

"Robin, what's going on?"

"How... could you make me *do this?*" I cried. The tears had begun flowing.

Alex came right up next to me and whispered, painfully, in my ear. "Robin, this is no time for games. Don't you understand how important this is? This is the favour. You have to do this. Benton is the Boss's most important client. Get in there."

I tore away from him. A couple of guys had arrived on the scene, presumably to keep me to my agreement. "You never said it was this! If I'd had known …" I felt two hands grip my arms. Benton was breathing heavily down my neck.

Alex came closer to me again. "You still would've taken the drugs. Robin, you have to pay him back. There's no other way." His voice was sad. I knew he, himself was torn with regret that he was trading his body for heroin. Benton started to pull me backward, but I reacted. I broke into a run and shoved past D, who was standing at the end of the hallway.

"Hey, boy! Where do you think…" his voice trailed off as I burst through the doors and out onto the cold street. I would not look back. I had reached my limit. Nothing could possibly be worth that. I ran as long as I could before I collapsed in a fit of coughing from the cold air rushing into my heaving lungs. I found an abandoned house on one of the street corners to shield myself from the wind and snow. Shivering, I zipped up my sweatshirt. I had left my coat in the hotel, and eyed the homeless man sleeping on the decaying stairs. My heart was wrenched. I knew that was going to be me. I found a room farther inside the rotten house that no one was squatting in and sat down in the cleanest spot I could find. I put my icy hand on my throbbing cheek, trying to soothe some of the pain. My stomach reeled as I felt Benton's hands on me. I leaned over just in time to vomit on the floor beside me instead of onto my lap. Shuddering, I curled up in the tightest ball I could and prayed; the only thing I could think of that might help me.

Jesus, I'm so scared. I know you've already helped me a lot, but if you could just help me one more time.

I jumped as a kid scooted in one of the windows and scampered through the room and out the other side of the house. Police sirens followed him. I started to sweat and shake. My drugs were wearing off, and I didn't have any left. I would never get any more either.

Jesus, please let me die right here. Make it quick. I don't want to suffer through this.

"Hey … you … share with a brother?" A dark shadow appeared in the dilapidated doorframe. I stayed as still as I could, hoping he would think I was dead. He rambled for a few minutes, but I couldn't understand his slurred words. He left, and I breathed shallow breaths, knowing that Jesus would probably not grant my request and kill me. I would have to live through withdrawal.

Jesus, if you won't let me die, save me. I need Israel. Please. Let Israel come. Let Israel come.

I don't know how much time passed, but every minute was more agonizing than the first. It got colder and colder, and I felt sicker and sicker. My blood started to race through my body, and it never stopped. Spots appeared in front of my eyes. I thought they were bugs and I panicked, scratching at my skin and clawing away at my clothes. Weird noises echoed in the garbage-filled room, and I didn't even realize it was me that was making them. I began to have delusions.

Robin … sweetie, it's time for school!

"Mom," I moaned. "I'm too sick to go to school." I sobbed an empty, dry sob. I knew she wasn't there. I knew she was dead and gone.

Get away from me! Every time I look at you, I see her! I don't want to see her! Get away from me! Every time I look at you, I see her! Get away from me …

I clamped my hands over my frozen ears in vain attempt to block out my father's hurtful words. "I'm sorry … sorry …" I whined. My body convulsed, and I threw up again.

Nothing but a menace. Delinquent. Ungrateful teenager. Only cares about himself. It's no wonder nobody wants him.

My blood raced faster as I writhed on the dirty floor.

Why are you still here? Shouldn't you have killed yourself already and done the world a favour?

"I … tried …" Tears streaming from my eyes, nose running … it felt like my face was bleeding.

Get out! I cannot inflict you on my family any longer!

"Israel!" I screamed. "Israel!" *Jesus, please bring him to me! Please!*

Warm hands scooped me up and held me tight. "I'm here, Robin. Israel's here, and I'll never let you go."

SACRIFICE

I couldn't decide if he was real or if he was just another one of my withdrawal symptoms. Shaking, I strained to see his face. "I prayed so hard … that you would—," a violent cough interrupted my ramblings, "—you would c … come." I felt one of his tears fall on my sweaty forehead.

Israel resituated himself on the dirty floor so he was closer to me. "I prayed so hard that I would find you," he said, struggling not to break down. "Oh, Robin, what have you done to yourself?"

I twitched as I thought of Benton again, his hands on me, pressing me into the floor, his lips inches away from mine. "How—how did you find me?" I clung to Israel's coat as I tried to force the memories to fade.

"Grandpa told me where he sent you, and when I found you weren't there, I talked to Alex's mom and found out you had taken off for the city. Now I know what kind of a person Alex is, so I had a general idea of where you were … but mostly, God led me straight to you. He knew you needed me."

I started to cry. A city of two million people, and he just happened to find the one broken-down house that I was dying in. I figured God must really care about me.

"Shhh," Israel said as he rubbed my shivering arms. "It's okay now... I got you."

I was shaking badly by then, and the tiny black spots had begun to swarm again. "You... wouldn't h-happen to h-have any... drugs-s-s for me, would you?" I asked in a final, futile attempt that I knew would not pull through for me. I think I even managed a small laugh after I had finished asking.

Israel's comforting hands rubbed the back of my neck. "No, Robin... I don't."

"I didn't t-think s-so." I could feel the surge of pain about ten seconds before it happened. It coursed through my entire body, contorting it into disgusting shapes. I scraped my fingers against the concrete walls as I clawed for something, anything to dull the ache.

"You could've died," Israel said.

"I st-still c-could," I stuttered through clenched teeth.

"No. No. God has a plan for your life. That's why he hit you so hard. He loves you. He wants you."

"I... know." I could feel him. I could feel God just waiting for me to let him into the empty hole I had inside me. "I know, I'm... s-sorry."

"You remember that story I told you? About the son who had returned to his father after wasting away his inheritance?"

I remembered the story.

"He's you. Robin, just come to Jesus. He's waiting for you with open arms, no matter how many bad things you've done. Ask him now. Ask him into your life," Israel urged.

How could I not? God had spared me and brought me Israel. I was a complete and total failure, and yet he still chased me. He still wanted me. Loved me. I prayed right then and there. I don't know how much sense it made; I couldn't really think straight, but in my heart, it was all I needed.

Israel tried to stand up. "I'll take you home," he said.

I couldn't move. I could barely think or even breathe. I know I wasn't coherent, because we never ended up going home. We stayed all night on that floor in the broken-down house, me writing in pain and Israel watching helplessly. All I can remember is how I felt, not what actually happened. The first thing that happened was my mutant heart and diseased soul finally healed. As soon as I made the commitment to God, I felt him wipe me clean. It was amazing, but the feeling didn't last for long. Eventually, I felt that my insides were being ripped out through my throat and nose, a dozen knives were stabbing me again and again all over my body, and someone had replaced all the liquid in my body with fire. Kind of like when the demon made me feel like I was being burned at the stake.

Israel prayed as I cried and screamed for hours. I tried to hit him, crawl away from him, and eventually I think I asked him to kill me, but all the while, Israel just prayed and held me tightly. Little by little, I stopped vomiting all over myself, and I stopped shaking. The sun streamed through the crumbling walls, and the barely-there windows as I drifted into a somewhat comatose-like state. I don't know how long I slept on that floor, completely spent and closer to death than either of us realized. I eventually opened my bloodshot eyes to a pile of garbage in front of me, the rancid smell of vomit under my nose. I tried to move, but I didn't get very far.

"How do you feel?" Israel asked.

I couldn't talk. My throat was as dry as a desert. Every time I moved my head, pain shot through my neck. I couldn't even feel my fingers or toes from the cold. Israel lifted me up off his lap and stood. I felt his strong hands grip me under my arms and gently stand me up.

"I can't carry you. You have to help me."

I had enough energy to focus on his face. Pale and sleep deprived, his face held only love for me. I reached for him, and he put my arm around his shoulder, but I had only moved a few feet when Israel stopped. I forced myself to lift my head up and look. A man was entering the building. He was one of the men I had seen in the hallway of the run-down motel. He was coming to collect on the debt I still owed. Israel didn't know what was going on, so he just stayed put, hoping the man had nothing to do with us. But I knew better. Even in my weakened state, I knew who he was and what was going to happen. I prayed to my God for another miraculous salvation.

"You little brat," the man growled, the tattoos on his neck pulsing. "Do you know how long I've been looking for you?" He stepped through the doorway of "my" room and shuffled past the heaps of garbage. He reached for me, but Israel stepped in front and pushed me back. I almost fell. "What are you doing? This kid has a debt to pay! Who are you?" The man's nostrils flared; his fingers itched for his side pocket. My heart stopped at the thought of what he wanted to reach for. I expected Israel to say something in my defence, but he didn't. He just kept pushing me back.

"Look..." the man said, scratching at his bald, snow-covered head. "I'm just going to be honest with you because I'm an honest guy." He smiled and pulled out of his pocket exactly what I had feared. Waving the gun in the air, he continued, "I'm exhausted. I'm frozen. I'm frickin' sick and tired of chasing these stupid kids who dine and dash. So either you hand him over..." he motioned to me with his gun; my gag reflex tried to take over again, "or... I'll shoot you in the face."

I felt Israel's body tremble, and I didn't think it was because of the cold.

"Well?" His black eyes narrowed. "What's it gonna be, pretty boy?" He raised the gun and pointed it straight at Israel's chest.

Israel still said nothing. I knew he was praying. So was I.

The bald man shuffled on his feet and sighed. "Oh, come on! If that doesn't motivate you..." All of a sudden, the gun was aiming at me. I closed my burning eyes to wait for the impact, but it didn't come. Instead, I was violently pushed even farther back, as Israel had apparently swatted the gun out of the man's hand. I opened my eyes from my position on the floor just in time to see Israel crumble under the blow of the man's fist.

"Freakin' punk," the man grumbled as his eyes left Israel and turned to me. "Get up, kid. You've got a debt to pay." He grabbed me by the front of my sweatshirt and pulled. I flew up into the air as he hoisted me with an incredible amount of strength, and tried to get my footing. I wanted to walk to my death. My memories were flooding past my eyes. Imminent death preceded by a period of torture seemed to bring them out. I could only imagine what they would do to me once they got me back to that motel.

The man dragged me outside, through two rancid rooms and past the homeless man on the steps. I could feel my body fight back. I tried to resist him, tried to pull and get away, grab onto anything I could reach, but it was futile. He was too strong, and I was too sick.

"Stop!" A voice yelled. I could barely hear it through my distress. "Wait!" A hand yanked the man's grip off me and pushed me to the ground.

"What the f—," the man started as he raised his gun to bring a devastating blow down on Israel's head.

"Please!" Israel yelled and put up his hands. "Please … "

The man paused.

Israel looked down at me, shivering in the snow. I watched him. All the fear was gone.

"Please," Israel pleaded. "Take me instead."

I immediately started to protest, but none of my words seemed to be audible. I clawed at Israel's legs, but he didn't acknowledge me.

The man just looked at Israel with a mocking and confused expression. "You instead of him? Don't you know what he owes?"

I heard Israel say yes, and I heard the man laugh. But the man's laughter died quickly as he realized Israel was actually serious. The wet snow started to seep into my clothes, and I panicked as reality was starting to set in.

The man was quiet for a few seconds. The only sounds I heard were Israel's heavy breathing and my own choked sobs. "So … you would … take his place, even though *you* didn't do anything?"

I heard Israel say yes again, but I tried to convince myself that he had actually said no.

The man kept the gun pointed at Israel and continued to

talk to him, but his eyes watched me. "What is your name?" he asked.

"Israel," came my cousin's strong reply.

"Israel," the man repeated with wonder. He motioned with his head for Israel to get into his car.

"Wh-what are you doing?" my anguished voice asked as I reached out for Israel.

He knelt down in the snow and lifted me up. "You're getting in the truck," he said, dragging me toward the old, familiar, rusty vehicle.

"Are we going home?" I managed to ask.

Israel grunted a little as he shoved me inside the cab. He grabbed my neck and pulled me into a desperate hug. "Yes ... yes, Robin, we are both going home." He kissed me on the forehead, and I felt his tears trickle down my face. He slammed the door shut and disappeared in the backseat of the man's car.

"What? Israel! Where are you going? *Why are you leaving me?*" I tried to open the door, but the handle wouldn't lift. I pounded on the frosted window with my frozen hands, my breath fogged up the glass. I was left alone, cold, exhausted, and sick. Shivering violently, I wailed and pulled my hair as my eyes frantically and hysterically searched for the car that was no longer there.

God... why is he gone? Why is he doing this? Please let him come back. Don't let him do this.

I don't know how much time passed, but with every second, I could feel less and less of my body. I tried to throw up again, but nothing was left inside my stomach to come out.

I'm going to die. God. Please. Where are you now?

There had been times where I had felt so sick I could barely move, or so much in pain I could barely think, but I had never felt myself dying before. It was as if there were a weight on me getting heavier by the second. I actually started to feel warmer. Slowly, I stopped moving. My eyes were going black. Slowly, I stopped crying. My heart was calming down. Slowly ... I stopped breathing.

NO GREATER LOVE

How is he?

His body temperature is almost normal now. He should be all right. There is the matter of his withdrawal, though. It's going be rough.

Can we take him home? Can't he—go through that at home?

No. We have to keep him under constant surveillance. There are certain complications that might arise from the hypothermia, such as kidney failure or heart irregularities.

Oh no…

We're hoping that doesn't happen, but we need to keep an eye on him. He'll be fine here. We'll make him as comfortable as we can. You can stay with him.

When do you think he'll wake up? When will the symptoms start?

We can't say for sure. It's different for every case. He's not in a coma, so he should wake up when his body has naturally rested itself. As for the withdrawal symptoms, they've already begun. We believe he suffered the first wave last night.

Is he in pain?

Not yet.

And when he wakes up?

It will start.

Can I sit with him?

Of course, Mrs. Neufeldt. I'll be back to check on him every once and a while.

I strained my ears to decipher what I was hearing. I felt like earplugs were crammed deep inside my head. I took a deep breath. The weight on my body had been lifted, but my throat was raw. I had no strength to cough. I wanted to see what was going on. It took all of my energy to pull my eyelids up only to feel as if I were in a movie theatre with no glasses on. I asked where I was, but I didn't hear the words.

"Doctor! Doctor, come quick! His eyes are open!"

I saw a blurry shape leaning over me. I felt a warm touch on my forehead.

"Robin … Sweetie, can you hear me?"

Where was Israel? I wanted to see him. I wanted him to hold onto me. I asked for him, but again, I didn't hear the words.

"Robin, if you can hear me and understand what I am saying, I want you to squeeze my hand."

A hand grasped mine. I held on tight. I knew it was Israel. He had come to take care of me.

"He squeezed my hand. He's coherent."

"Robin! Sweetie! Oh, can you hear me?"

Her voice trailed off as I slipped back into my deep sleep. I had used up all the energy I had been able to create. I knew who she was, but I couldn't say her name in my mind. I couldn't figure out a lot of things in my mind. It was as if the ideas and thoughts would get so close to my grasp and then dart away before I could grab them. I stopped trying. Maybe if I slept some more.

My eyes opened. I stared at my blurry movie screen for a few minutes, trying to focus on something, anything. Finally, the picture on the wall went from a blob of color to a vase of flowers. I took another deep breath and looked around the room. I had been in hospitals for years of my life but never from the perspective of the patient. I immediately wanted out. I tried to move, but I couldn't. At first, I thought I was too weak, but then when

I glanced down I noticed my arms were strapped into the bed. I flexed my muscles against them just once and then gave up when my energy level dropped about 50 percent. My strained eyes drifted over to the window. I saw a beautiful sky of pink and orange. The sunset. It warmed my heart to see the incredible colors God could put in the sky. He didn't have to make it beautiful if he didn't want to, but he did. I knew he put it there just for me. As I focused on breathing deeper, my eyesight got clearer. I saw a nurse walk by the glass window. I looked right at her until she saw me and came in. Her precious smile made me calm. She was the most beautiful thing I had ever seen. Blonde hair. Fair skin. She looked almost exactly like my mother.

"Good evening," her voice soothed. "It's nice to see you awake." Her hand stroked my cheek and felt my forehead. "Does it hurt anywhere?"

I managed to shake my head no. I couldn't take my eyes off her.

"Good. I'm going to take these straps off now, okay? Just relax." She started to undo them, but she kept her eyes on me. "You're wondering what's going on, aren't you? I can see it in your eyes." She smiled her calming smile and moved to the other side of the bed to undo my other strap. "Severe hypothermia. That means you almost froze to death. We had to warm you up and keep you as still as possible. That's why we put these on you. Just a safety measure."

I looked down at my now free arms. It felt good to be able to move them, but my momentary happiness faded when I saw the track marks in my skin. I gently ran my fingers over the raised lines. I could feel the needles inside again. Flinching, I jerked my other hand away. The nurse caught it.

"Hey…" She held my hand tight in both of hers. "Don't think about that. That's over. This is your second chance. I know you won't screw it up." She smiled and left, thinking she had left me feeling relaxed. But she was wrong.

The thoughts that had been escaping me finally let me catch them. All at once. I felt the needles digging into my arms, the drugs itching at my nose. I felt Alex's fists beat at my face; I tasted the toilet water. I felt the demons claw at my legs and Benton's hands all over my body. My muscles contorted. I leaned over the guardrail on my hospital bed. I saw my tears make little splash marks on the linoleum floor. My knuckles burned and turned white as I gripped the bars.

Jesus! Help me ... I can't do this! I can't think about these things! Help me!

"Robin!" I heard a small voice exclaim. I couldn't acknowledge it. I was leaning over the bed, fighting my own regrets and trying to suppress the inevitable tremors of the withdrawal that wasn't even close to being over, even though I thought it was. Mumbling, whining, and shuffling occurred, and then I felt strong hands take my shoulders. Eli was holding me, and Martha's face appeared beside me.

"God, our Father in heaven," Eli's voice rang. "Release Robin from this anxiety. Calm his spirit. Quench his soul." Martha stroked my hair as I continued to shake and weep silent tears over my bed railing. Eli kept praying, and slowly, I felt God's peace enter my heart and wipe my mind of the things that tormented me. I was able to lie back and recover emotionally. Martha's tear-streaked face smiled comfort at me and sat on the side of my bed. My thoughts were still there, but now there was a wall holding them back from torturing me.

"It's going to be okay now, Robin. We're here," Martha said, holding my hand in hers. I looked at Eli. His eyes held love, regret, and fear. I knew all three well.

"Don't mind my intrusion," the doctor said as he entered the room, his sights set on me.

Eli stood up and backed away so the doctor could approach me.

"Robin, my name is Jerry." His kind eyes smiled as he spoke. "How do you feel?"

"I—," my voice cracked. I felt like there was an invisible force holding back the shakes, the seizures, the convulsions that were aching to erupt. "It's not over, is it?"

"No, it's not. Are you in any specific pain right now?"

I wanted to tell him that my heart and soul hurt, but I didn't think that's what he had meant. "No."

Jerry hung the clipboard back on the hook at the foot of my bed and looked me in the eye. "I don't know how long it's going to last, Robin, but it's not going to be easy. We're going to try and make you as comfortable as we can for as long as it takes, okay?"

I was terrified. I knew it wasn't gone, I knew there was more to come, but I thought it would be easier. I thought it wouldn't be as bad. "You mean, the worst isn't over?"

"I'm sorry," he said, his eyes telling me those words had been spoken thousands of times, each time losing more of their meaning. "I'll be around if you need me for the next hour, and then Dr. Olsen will be taking the night shift."

Eli shook hands with Jerry earnestly. "Thank you."

I turned my slowly fading attention back to Martha. "Where's Israel?"

Before she could answer, Caleb, Esther, and Eve all timidly snuck into the room and inched up to my bed. Caleb put his little hand on my arm and smiled. "Hi, Robin. I'm glad you're okay."

My heart wanted to break. This little kid was staring at the one who almost killed him, and still he was feeling compassion and showing love. "Thanks," I managed to squeak out without bursting into tears. The girls didn't say anything, but their eyes showed the same fear for my life. I wanted to talk more; I wanted to hug them all and tell them that I loved them, but my eyes refused to stay open. I heard Martha usher them out and tell them that I needed to sleep. I was still suffering the effects of the hypothermia. Martha stayed next to me while I dreamed.

I didn't really dream about a specific time or place; I just dreamed about them: Marcus and Tiffany Cane, my mom and my dad. I dreamed of my house in Miami. My mom was standing at her easel, painting a picture of the flower vase on the table, much similar to the one in the painting on my hospital room wall. Her shining blonde hair reflected the sunlight streaming in through the open window. She hummed quietly to herself, knowing that her husband would soon be home and in her arms. She loved him so much. I stayed hidden behind the living room wall. I didn't want her to see me the way I was. I didn't want her to see me as a failure. My dad came home and scooped her up in his arms. Her squeal of delight echoed in my aching ears as their happiness overwhelmed me in my grief. I knew none of it was real. I knew none of it was happening, but they turned and called to me. Their eyes loved me as they once had done so long ago, and it didn't matter if I was wretched and guilty; they still held out their arms to me. I ran to them and fell into their embrace. I cried and cried as they hugged and kissed me, but they were tears of joy. The only thing I had ever wanted was to hold them again, to see her one last time, and to know that he loved me.

And just as quickly as it had come, it was gone. I was in my hospital bed, my eyes were dry, and I was alone. At least I thought I was alone. I didn't notice the old man sitting in an armchair in the corner of the room. I only looked around when I smelled his aftershave. He was just staring right at me, as if he were waiting on pins and needles for me to wake up. As soon as I looked over at him, he rose from his chair and shuffled to my bed, dragging his wooden chess box with him. He sat down in the chair next to me and pushed the button on my bed to make my head rise up. The bed whirred and whistled as Grandpa Joe set up his chess pieces. To my surprise, I was excited. Chess required thinking, and if I was thinking about strategy, I wouldn't be thinking about anything else, especially the strange feeling that had started to form inside my stomach. I tried to sit up a bit with the ounce of strength I had. I saw his eyes dart down for a split second and then back at his black pieces. I knew what he saw. He saw the purple and red lines in my arm. Shamefully, I pulled the bed sheet over my arm and proceeded to concentrate on the game as best I could. My mind would often wander, and so he got the best of me right away. I couldn't help but think about how I got from the truck to the hospital, or where Israel was, or what had happened to Alex, or how much longer it would be before the symptoms hit me again. Sweat was already forming on my forehead.

Once Grandpa had captured my queen, I asked him. "How did I get here?"

He grunted and started to chase after my king, the only piece I had left. "Put out an APB on the truck. Cops picked it up, found you inside." He knocked over my king and looked up at my face. "You were almost dead when they brought you in. The good Lord was watching over you, boy."

I swallowed. I knew that already. I had felt my body die. "I know. I've lost track of how many times he's saved me."

A small smile twitched on Grandpa's lips as he put away his game.

My head flopped back on the pillow. The strange feeling in my stomach was turning into a sharp pain of desire. "Where's Israel?"

Grandpa stood up and put his rattling game box on the side table. "The family will be back any minute."

I was about to ask again when Eli and Martha appeared in the doorway, followed by two police officers.

"Robin..." Martha waddled to me and planted a warm kiss on my cheek. "It's a miracle to see you so awake." She stepped back so Eli could greet me. My first gut reaction was to back away from him. The last time I had seen him he looked as if he wanted to kill me with his bare hands. But he squeezed my shoulder and smiled reassuringly.

"How you doing?" he asked.

My blood pressure spike declined. "Okay."

Eli took off his ball cap and motioned to the officers standing at the foot of my bed. "This is Portman and Blanche. They're from the EPS. Edmonton Police Service. They need to take a statement from you."

I thought I knew why, but I couldn't quite pull all the facts together. My mind was starting to fail me. "Um...why?"

Martha and Eli looked at each other sadly. Grandpa Joe remained stoic.

"Robin," Eli began, "Israel's missing. You were the last person to see him."

My hands started to go cold. "How ... do you know I was the last?"

Martha turned away to hide her tears.

"Israel took the truck to come after you. You were in the truck, so he must have found you. You must've seen what happened to him," Eli pleaded.

With a few blank spots, I could see the entire story as it happened, as if someone had laid out the plot outline for me. My fizzing mind was giving me its last ounce of strength. I closed my eyes as my mind started to relive every experience.

"Robin," Portman said as he approached me, "did you see where he went? Did you see what happened? Did he tell you where he was going?"

I could barely remember what Israel had said when he shoved me into the truck; I had been in so much pain. But there was one thing I knew for sure. "Someone took him away," I said, each word more agonizing to say than the last.

"Who?" Blanche prodded, scribbling in his notebook.

Martha took my hand. Only against the steadiness of her hand did I notice the shakiness of mine. "Um ... I don't know who it was ... some guy from ... " It felt like another one of those ideas that was just out of my reach. I was trying to grab it, trying to focus on it, and then like a bolt of lightning, it hit me. They guy who took him was coming to kill me, but he took Israel instead.

"From where?" they demanded.

I knew I had to explain to them. If I didn't, they might not get Israel back. I tried so hard to stay calm against the emerging anxieties. I tried so hard to say the words that stabbed me. "After ... I left the house ... I went to stay with Alex." I felt my body trying to convulse. I forced it not to. "He's the one who ... uh ... "

"He was your supplier. We know that much," Portman interrupted. "He's missing too."

Another wave of shame swept over me. Martha urged me on.

"Um ... I stayed with him at his house. He gave me ... " I didn't even have to say it. Everyone already knew. "He told me we had to go into the city to pay the guy who he got the stuff from. So we went. I don't really know ... I was high ... " I wanted to bury my head in the ground I was so ashamed.

Eli took my hand. "Robin ... that's in the past now. Come on ... concentrate. This is important."

I nodded and continued pushing my failing mind. "He took me to this ... place ... a motel ... there were other boys there." My muscles froze up. Benton might as well have just walked into the room right then.

Martha's eyes brimmed with tears. "Are you okay? What happened at the motel?"

I started to choke on tears of my own as I continued my story. "They took me to a room ... I was supposed to pay my debt ... there was a man there." My sobs broke up my words. I trembled for a few moments, but Martha's loving arms helped me get control of my emotions. "He grabbed me and threw me onto the bed," I whispered. "But I got out of there! I ran as fast as I could!" I yelled while still clutching Martha. Eli grunted in disgust.

"How far did you run?" Blanche asked, looking up from his scribbling.

My eyes were locked straight ahead. I was in somewhat of a trance. "Not far. I found an old house ... "

"The same one we found you in front of?" Portman nodded to Blanche, who quickly exited, chattering excitedly on his radio. "Then what happened, Robin?"

"I got sick. I didn't have any drugs. Israel found me. He stayed with me. He put me in the truck."

Eli shuffled on his feet as Portman wrote more notes to himself. I hoped he wouldn't ask me any more questions, but I knew he would ask one more. I knew what it was too ... and I didn't want to answer it.

"Robin, where is Israel?"

My eyes were dry. My heartbeat was rising. My grip was death on Martha's arms. "They came for me. They took him instead."

I heard Martha gasp, but she didn't leave my side.

"Why?" Portman asked.

The scene came flooding back into my mind. The man dragging me through the snow. Israel pulling me away. The man's laughter. Israel's plea. My cries.

Eli knew why. He turned away from us and went to stand at the wall. I heard him cry.

"Robin!" Martha finally lost it. "*Why did they take my baby?*" She shook me hard. My heart broke again as I looked into her red face. I knew my next words would hurt her.

"He took my place. He told the man to take him instead of me."

She screamed. Suddenly my eyes blacked out again. My burning cheek told me she had slapped me with all the grief a mother should never have. I didn't blame her. I watched as Eli comforted Martha as she sobbed horrid tears. My heart bled for them. The police officer said something to me and then left, but I didn't even hear him. My exhausted frame fell back on the bed, beads of sweat trickling down my skin. I prayed harder than I'd ever prayed before. I needed Israel to be okay. I needed him to come back.

WAITING FOR MY WORLD TO CHANGE

After Martha had slapped me and fallen to the floor in a fit of sobs, it started. It began slowly, causing me to toss and turn, fidget restlessly. I started shivering, every muscle in my body began to ache, pains attacked my insides. I felt like I was starving, dying of thirst. Every breath took immense effort. I had no physical strength, and yet I kept going; I kept thrashing. With every passing minute, my agony got worse. Light burned my eyes, sound stabbed at my ears, touch scraped my skin. For two days I suffered. Two whole days Martha and Eli took turns sitting with me, praying for me as my body struggled to function without the drug I had infected it with. Remember I told you how I thought being in my little Podunk town with relatives that I hated was hell on earth? I couldn't have been more wrong. Those two days of withdrawal were my hell on earth. I don't know how else I can describe it to you. I can't even tell you that after those two days, my symptoms just died down and I fell into a peaceful sleep, because that's not what happened. Yes, my symptoms died down, but I didn't sleep. I couldn't. Apparently, one of the symptoms of withdrawal is insomnia. I remember lying there on those sweaty, rumpled sheets, knowing that it was over and knowing that I had made it, but also knowing that the knowledge of victory was the only reward I was going to get.

Once I had been coherent for a while, Eli came in and explained to me what was going on.

There was no trace of Israel anywhere. The cops had found the hotel where they were dealing drugs and pimping and shut it down. They also said they had their best men on the case looking for Israel, but there was no way to be sure, seeing as how they were also going after D and the boss. We just had to trust them. We had to trust God.

The day of my release took its time. I stayed in my bed with nothing but my own guilt, my aches and pains, and my insomnia. If I thought I had been burning alive before, I didn't know what to think about the way I felt then. Maybe drowning in my own despair for hours on end. I had a hard time breathing. There was a constant pool of water on my chest from my tears, and my body felt so heavily laden and wasted, I could barely move. When Eli and Martha finally arrived to take me back to their house, I almost couldn't care less if they left me there forever. I looked up expecting to see Eli, but it was Martha who entered my room. By herself. She stared at the floor for a few moments and then waddled over to me, clutching her purse for dear life.

"Robin," she stammered, "I wanted to talk to you alone for a moment."

I forced myself out of the deep end and gave her my full attention.

She took one of my hands and rubbed it gently. "I can never forgive myself for what I did … to you." Her pooling eyes met mine. "I have no excuse … just my sincerest apology. I hope I didn't hurt you too much." Her lips quivering, she paused.

All of a sudden, I was overwhelmed with love for her. I squeezed her hand.

"Now I know I could never replace … your mother … but … I want to be there for you. I want to be your friend. Do you think…do you think that would be okay?" Her grasp on my hand turned desperate.

The tears started to come again, but for a different reason. Why had I scorned this beautiful woman? Why had I hurt her? Why did I push her away? All along, I had someone to care for me and guide me, and I had refused her. My anger and bitterness had completely ruined my life, and I was determined to change.

"Oh, sweetie…" she cooed, wiping my tears away. I reached out for her, and we hugged for the longest time. "I love you, you know that?" she said.

"I love you too," came my whispered and nervous voice. I hadn't said those words since my mom died, but my heart soared as I held onto Martha. I thanked God for her a thousand times.

The nurse brought me my clothes, and as difficult as it was to get dressed, I managed. I thanked God again for my health. For my life. I couldn't stop thanking him; he was on my mind constantly. The desire for him had replaced the desire for drugs. Unfortunately, he couldn't take my fear away. He couldn't make Israel appear right in front of me. Well, he could if he wanted to, but I knew he wouldn't. He didn't just snap his fingers and fix everything; he had his own plan, and not being too experienced in the ways of trusting God, I still wallowed in despair.

I kind of let them push and pull me wherever they wanted me to go. I didn't care if I had my coat on when I went outside. I didn't care if I had my seatbelt on as we drove back to the farm. I didn't care that an awkward silence engulfed me and my family throughout the entire ride. I only cared about Israel, if the cops were doing their best, if it wasn't too late, and if God was still watching out for him. Did he know that I needed him? Did God know I wanted him back? I didn't know if I was supposed to beg God for Israel's safe return, or if I was supposed to wait. I think I begged.

When we arrived, Martha helped me out of the car and led me to the house.

"Robin…" Eli said suddenly.

I turned to look.

"There aren't any more drugs in your room, are there?" he asked unwillingly.

Martha started to scold him for asking at such a sensitive time, but I answered right away. I wanted him to know that everything would be fine, that I would never touch drugs again, not after what I had just been through. "No. No, there's nothing in there."

He nodded, put his arm around my other shoulder, and helped Martha lead me inside. They took me to the living room, and I stayed there. For hours. Curled up in the corner of the sofa, I thought, prayed, and tried to forget about my aching body. My past sins and mistakes usually liked to come and hit me in the face, but this time it was different. This time, instead of beating myself up over them, my mind began to think of ways to set things right. I could call Justin back in Miami, apologize and tell him I missed him. I could contact Alice, say sorry for throwing macaroni in her face and scaring her to death, and thank her for all my garbage she put up with. Pay Bret back for damaging his Mountie, Peace Officer car. Apologize to the seniors at school I beat up. Try to build a relationship with Peter after he forgave me for everything. The list didn't stop there, but my awareness did. Finally, after who knows how many hours it had been since I had last slept, I drifted to sleep. I eventually woke up in the midst of total silence. The single lamp on the corner table cast a dim light into the empty, ancient living room. I stretched out on the floral sofa. My legs tingled as the blood flowed back into them. Falling asleep all crunched up was not the best idea, but since it had been so long, I was grateful for what I got. As my legs were stinging, my heart skipped a beat. There was someone sitting in the armchair next to me. Heavy breathing came from underneath a baseball cap, penetrating the total silence of the room.

"Peter?" I said, not really quite sure if it was him or if I was seeing things.

He pushed his hat to the side so he could see me. "Hey... I guess I fell asleep while I was waiting for you to wake up."

I ran my fingers through my long, clean, gel-less hair and

leaned over, stretching out my back. "How long have you been here?"

He yawned and brought his legs up underneath him. "A few hours."

"You could've woke me."

"Nah, it's okay. I was talking with someone else anyway." He smiled.

"I bet you didn't get an answer either," my tired voice said. Leaning back, I watched him as his smile faded.

"No." He shook his head sadly. "I didn't get an answer either. Not about that." He leaned forward. "But I did get an answer about something else. I've been praying you into the kingdom ever since I met you, Cane ... and here you are." He extended his hand to me, and I grasped it fervently.

I told myself not to cry before I spoke. "I couldn't have survived without him. I just wish it wouldn't have taken me this long."

"The evil one had a strong, strong hold on you. I'm surprised it didn't take you longer." Peter squeezed my arm. "And you and I both know if it had taken longer, you wouldn't be here."

I could feel the tears coming. I desperately fought them. I didn't want to cry again, especially in front of Peter. "But ... if I hadn't been so blind ... so stubborn ... Israel wouldn't have had to—"

"God put Israel here for that very purpose! You can't live on *what ifs*. This is the path you took. You'll never know if you would have done it differently or not, but the grace of God is what got you down the path you chose! You were on your way to destruction, but God placed Israel in your life to stop you, to turn you around."

I controlled my emotions by looking away from Peter. "I know ... I know he did ... but what if ... one life for another isn't—"

"And why not? That's what love is. Jesus died on the cross for the same reason." Peter looked into my eyes with truth and confidence. "Israel knows where he's going when he dies. He's not afraid."

I knew that too. Israel had said it clearly when he left me. I laughed a small awkward laugh. "When I asked him where he was going, he said he was going home—" My voice stopped. "I guess I didn't understand what he meant." Looking down at my lap again, I tried once more to control the torrent of emotions that threatened to spill.

Peter and I talked into the wee hours of the morning about God and salvation. He brought out his Bible and I grabbed it, earnestly flipping through the pages, anxious to read every word of it. I had so many questions about everything. He did his best to answer me, to reassure me, and when we talked about the devil and demonic powers, I expected the old familiar trapped feeling to resurface, but instead I felt strong and pure. As the sun came up, I fell more and more in love with Jesus. I had never felt that way before. So peaceful, so protected, so redeemed. God loved me even though I hurt my family, my friends, and even strangers. He loved me even though I stole, did drugs, and cursed his name. He hunted me down, chased me, and finally caught me. It felt good to be in the arms of someone who cared that much. I was almost to the point where I felt like nothing could ever go wrong again, but then it happened. Someone banged on the front door.

It was 7:34 in the morning when they told us Israel was dead. They found his body on the side of the road a couple of miles from the city. I had just reached the conclusion that God would protect Israel. He would keep him safe and bring him back because he was a good and loving God ... but he didn't. I didn't know what to think. Martha started sobbing as she slid down into one of the chairs at the kitchen table, and I watched her. It felt like I didn't even know what she was doing. It was like my brain didn't recognize tears or sorrow. I looked over at Eli, who was still talking with George. He was pale but calm. My mind didn't understand his emotional restraint. It was watching Peter crying silently into his hands that finally made me understand. I skirted around him and around Eli and George and took off outside. I ran sloppily through the melting snow and ice, tears rolling down my cheeks, my weak muscles threatening to give out. The cold air made me cough more violently than ever, and I had to slow down. I ended up where I had run off to the first night I had stayed at the farm. The night I had spent next to the hay bale. The night Bret had picked me up.

There had been many times in my life where I wanted to cry out to a god of some kind. I had always felt there was something there, but I had never known what it was. Now that I knew, I could cry out till my heart was content. I knew he didn't hate me. I knew he didn't want to see me suffer. He was my creator, my father, and my saviour. But that morning as I stood out in the wet field, shivering and weeping, I couldn't understand why God would let Israel die for me. Didn't he care about Israel? Sure, he used Israel as an instrument to bring me into his love, but what about Israel? Didn't he have a life to live? As I continued to stand, feet soaking, I finally came to a slow realization. Israel did live his life. He lived it exactly the way God wanted him to. God put Israel in place to save me. Israel, even though he died, was already saved. Israel gave up his life to give me one, and he was rewarded by joining Jesus in heaven. My tears didn't stop flowing, and my heart didn't stop breaking, but I knew that everything would eventually be okay. Israel did what he did because he loved me, and there was no way I was going to dishonour that. I would live my life to the fullest, doing *what* I don't know, but I wouldn't let it waste away, not after it had just cost so much.

I walked slowly back home to where the police car was just pulling away. All was quiet. I couldn't hear anything from inside the house. I looked over to Grandpa Joe's cabin. The front door was open, so I assumed he had gone inside the house to be with Eli and Martha. I didn't know what to do next. I was just about to head back out to the field when the front screen door screeched open. Peter stepped out, closely followed by Eli. Peter came to stand by me as Eli got into his vehicle and started the engine. The sound wasn't very loud, but it was loud enough to drown out my tiny words.

"What's going on?"

Eli pulled the van right up next to me on the gravel road and rolled down the window. "I'm going to the station to ... identify him ... make some arrangements in town." His stricken eyes met mine dead on. "Take care of Martha."

I nodded and he drove off, spraying mud and rocks everywhere.

Peter put his hand on my shoulder. "What do you need, Robin?"

I grasped his hand and sighed. "I need you to pray for me. Everything has changed. Everything."

He told me he would as a few more tears escaped his eyes. We hugged, and he left. I took a deep breath and headed for the house. I had no idea what to do, or what to expect, but I knew I wouldn't be alone.

THE END OF IT ALL

I sat on the side of his bed and squeezed out the last of my tears in my tissue. I didn't want to get my suit wet. I sighed and looked around the loft. January 27, 2008, the day of Israel's funeral. I didn't want to go. It would be my third funeral in two and a half years. The days preceding the funeral had been so sorrowful, so heavy, I didn't think I could bear the actual service. Even though my heart had been changed forever, my physical body was still trying to catch up. It didn't know how to deal with the pain, and the first instinct it put into my mind was to dull my senses with any kind of drug I could find. Fortunately, there were no drugs for me to even consider it. Instead, I would sit on my bed, read the Bible that Peter had given me, and try to dwell on the fact that God knew what he was doing and that he would take care of me. Peter was great. He would come around every so often to make sure I was okay. We would talk for a little, but then I would fall silent again, and he would leave, saying he'd come back later. And then the last time he had come, he told me the next time he'd see me would be at the funeral. I don't think my mind had taken the time to register that there would be another funeral I'd have to endure. And before my mind could register it, I was sitting on his bed, in our empty loft, in my black suit, just waiting till the time came to leave. I heard the van doors sliding outside in the yard, and I forced my legs to stand me up and move me toward the ladder. But before I could leave, something caught my eye. Israel's journal. Immediately I darted forward and snatched it up, flipping to the last entry.

I know Dad did the right thing in sending him away, even though it was hard for me to watch him go. Robin has to figure it out on his own. I know that now. But I also know that God is telling me to go find him. I know he's in trouble. I'm not telling Dad though. He won't let me go, but I know I have to. I know it. I know what kind of stuff he's gotten himself into, and I'm not afraid. I'd die before I'd let anything happen to him. I hope he knows that.

I didn't think my heart could break anymore, but after reading the last word he wrote, my heart shattered into a billion pieces. I closed the journal and hugged it to my chest.

"I know that now, Israel. I know it now," I whispered. I knew he heard me.

"Robin?" Eli's voice floated up to the loft. "It's time to go."

I gently put Israel's journal under my pillow and followed Eli out to the van. No one said a thing during the drive to the church. Martha didn't stop blowing her nose, and the kids barely breathed for fear of upsetting the sense of calm that had settled over the family. Grandpa Joe stared out the window, and Eli kept his eyes glued to the road, except for an occasional glance at me in the rear-view mirror. I wished I could tell what he was thinking.

Israel's funeral was the hardest funeral to get through in my entire life. I thought I had prepared myself mentally and spiritually, but nothing could've prepared me for the church to be packed with five hundred people, none with a dry eye. I sat in between Caleb and Peter, both of whom were sobbing just as much as me. Patrick had to pause multiple times in order to get a hold of his emotions. What he said about Israel was beautiful, and even though we were all in agony over his death, the service was more of a celebration of his life than a declaration of our loss. I liked it that way. I wouldn't have wanted it any other way.

When the time came to go to the gravesite, my feet couldn't possibly have stayed rooted to the spot more. Peter took my arm and gently but strongly led me outside to the little graveyard ten minutes away from the church. I felt inside my pocket for the rustle of the paper I had put in there earlier. Did I mention that Eli requested me to read what was on the paper at the funeral? He did... and he wouldn't let me read it beforehand. I never wanted to do anything against his wishes ever again, so I didn't read it.

As the crowd gathered at the site in the middle of the little cemetery, I tried to take my eyes off the coffin. Instead of black, it was white, and just covered in red roses. I looked over at my family. They had all been seated in the front line of the rows that were forming. Patrick stood in the middle, right next to Israel and beckoned me forward. I don't know where the strength came from, but I had enough to actually move to stand next to him.

"Go ahead," Patrick whispered as he stepped back. I was left alone, standing next to Israel in the middle of the precious friends and family who had gathered. With trembling hands, I pulled out the wrinkled paper from my pocket and looked for Peter. I spotted him off to the side. He nodded to say, "Go ahead. I'm here if you need me." I saw Lynnette, Alan, and a few others from the youth group all watching me and holding hands, waiting for me to speak. The last person I saw before bending my head to read the words was the little old lady who had hugged me in church. Her face shone brighter than the sun, and that gave me the energy to read.

"Do not stand at my grave and weep. I am not there; I do not sleep." My voice was surprisingly clear as it rang out the first few words of the poem. "I am a thousand winds that blow. I am the diamond glint on snow. I am the sunlight on ripened grain. I am the gentle autumn rain."

I paused, and I could see the glory of God resting on everyone at the gravesite.

"When you wake in the morning hush, I am the swift, uplifting rush of quiet birds in circling flight. I am the soft starlight at night."

My eyes scanned the last stanza. As I took in the words, they disappeared. My heart could no longer bear it. The last stanza I read in between weeping.

"Do not stand at my grave and weep ... I am ... not there; I do not sleep. Do not stand at my grave and c-cry ... "

My entire body started shaking. I didn't have the strength to finish. It was too painful. I put my hand up to cover my eyes. I couldn't look at their faces. I couldn't look at their tears. It was too much. But a pair of small arms wrapped around my waist. I looked down and saw Caleb's little face. It was all I needed to finish.

"I am not there. I did not die."

BEFORE I GO

My name is Robin Cane. I was sixteen years old. I was dead.

I lost everything. It wasn't my decision. My family, my home, my friends ... my reason for being ... my hope ... all gone. I attempted suicide so many times because I didn't know how to deal with it. I tried swallowing pills, I tried slitting my wrists, I tried shooting myself, and I even tried suicide by cop. Nothing worked. Every time, something stopped me from physically ending my life, and I still lived in constant pain. But once I started trying to kill myself inside, there was no one to stop me. I fell deeper and deeper into captivity and depression, pushing myself to a slow death, and I didn't even realize it. I put others in danger, as well as myself, even though I thought I was only subduing my grief. Everyone gave up on me. They finally had realized what I had known all along, that I was a lost cause ... not worth anything ... un-loved. But there was one who thought differently. He was good and loving, the perfect example of a son and of a friend. He saw something in me that no one else would take the time to see. He saw my rebellion, my hatred, but he looked right through it. He saw my decrepit soul and my tainted heart, and he knew I was a slave to them. His love was so great that he traded places with me. He took my destroyed and dead-ended life and gave me his to live instead. There is no greater love than that.

My name is Robin Cane. I am seventeen years old. I was saved.